Passage to Mythrin

THE RUBY KINGDOM

Passage to Mythrin

THE RUBY KINGDOM

Patricia Bow

A BOARDWALK BOOK
A MEMBER OF THE DUNDURN GROUP
TORONTO

Editor: Barry Jowett
Copy Editor: Jennifer Gallant
Design: Alison Carr
Printer: Webcom

Library and Archives Canada Cataloguing in Publication

Bow, Patricia, 1946-
The ruby kingdom / Patricia Bow.

ISBN-13: 978-1-55002-667-2
ISBN-10: 1-55002-667-4

I. Title.

PS8553.O8987R82 2007   jC813'.54   C2006-904614-X

1   2   3   4   5   10   09   08   07   06

We acknowledge the support of the **Canada Council for the Arts** and the **Ontario Arts Council** for our publishing program. We also acknowledge the financial support of the **Government of Canada** through the **Book Publishing Industry Development Program** and **The Association for the Export of Canadian Books**, and the **Government of Ontario** through the **Ontario Book Publishers Tax Credit program** and the **Ontario Media Development Corporation**.

Care has been taken to trace the ownership of copyright material used in this book. The author and the publisher welcome any information enabling them to rectify any references or credits in subsequent editions.

J. Kirk Howard, President

Printed and bound in Canada
Printed on recycled paper

www.dundurn.com

Dundurn Press	Gazelle Book Services Limited	Dundurn Press
3 Church Street, Suite 500	White Cross Mills	2250 Military Road
Toronto, Ontario, Canada	High Town, Lancaster, England	Tonawanda, NY
M5E 1M2	LA1 4XS	U.S.A. 14150

This book is for Vivian Katherine Bow,
who came with wings.

CHAPTER ONE
THE BLUE FLARE

Forever afterward they remembered it, all three of them, as the day when the world changed. But at the time, for Simon at least, it just looked like a really bad day. The first bad day in a long line of bad days to come.

He could pinpoint exactly the moment when things started to go downhill. It was at 2:15 p.m. on that first day, a Sunday between Christmas and New Year's, when Celeste got back from Pearson International Airport and the car door opened and his cousin Ammy slid out.

For a couple of seconds he didn't even know it *was* Ammy. It wasn't just that the clothes and the hair were different. It was everything else.

After getting out of the car she just slumped there, bare hands in the pockets of her short black leather jacket, chin sunk into the folds of a long red scarf wrapped around and around her neck. The tight jacket and jeans made her look thin as a stick, and the big lace-up boots made her feet look enormous. Her short hair stuck up in spikes all over her head, red with yellow tips. Not red or yellow like real hair. Red like a neon light. Yellow like ballpark mustard.

The last time he'd seen Ammy, on a visit to Vancouver with Celeste two years ago, she'd had normal hair, plain brown just like his. It was long then, and she'd worn it in a ponytail. He'd liked it like that. Now she looked like her head was on fire.

While Simon hauled a few hundred pounds of suitcases and backpacks and gym bags out of the trunk, Celeste whisked Ammy up to the apartment. To amuse her, they took the old elevator that looked like a square brass birdcage and creaked up to the second floor slower than you could walk. At no time did Ammy look amused.

At first, Simon put it down to her being tired. She'd flown all the way from Vancouver to Toronto, and then it was two hours by road to Dunstone. Even though somebody else had done all the piloting and driving and she'd just sat, he guessed she wouldn't be sparkling much.

And then, before he'd had time to duck out, Celeste handed him Ammy as a chore. Or, as she put it, a mission. "Make her feel at home," Celeste said. "Make her feel she belongs. I'm counting on you, kiddo."

He did try. He brought Ike Vogelsang along to help. They started with the new mall, which Simon had been sure would impress her. It had a CD store, and two clothing stores that kids at school said were cool — Simon himself was no judge — and a food court where you could get coffee out of a real Italian espresso machine with valves and dials and a brass eagle on top and buy stone-hard Italian cookies to dunk. He bought her one, and a coffee to dunk it in.

"Very nice," Ammy said. "Thank you very much." She drank the coffee all at one go but left the cookie uneaten. Ike claimed it. "Please do," Ammy said, and she smiled, but her eyes were like two blue lights that never got switched on.

She said "Thank you" and "Very nice" at every turn. But she hardly said anything else. That was a clue, Simon realized later. The Ammy he remembered — well, you couldn't shut her up. And she hadn't been especially polite.

Ike had the bright idea of showing her Dunstone Public School, where she would go for the next six months while her parents, who were engineers, were working in South America. She and Ike and Simon would all be in grade eight together. "It's not a bad school," Ike said. "You'll make friends." He grinned at her. Combined with the freckles, the grin was usually effective. Not this time.

Ammy looked at the red-brick shoebox with no expression at all. "Very nice."

Ike and Simon exchanged glances and minuscule shrugs. "What's with her?" Ike muttered, as she trudged ahead of them up the street. "You said she was fun."

"She used to be." Simon kicked at a knob of ice and sent it skittering.

"Maybe you don't know her all that well."

"She's my cousin! I've known her forever."

"One visit a year is not forever."

"It's like she's a different person."

"Maybe she is." Ike brightened. "Maybe the real Ammy's been snatched by aliens."

"I wish this one would be."

They ended up in front of Quasars, Simon's favourite store, at dusk. The store windows all along Bain Street were ablaze with Christmas lights.

"This place is really neat," Simon said, stubbornly cheerful. "There's millions of games and kits and models in there. You can make your own … um…" He waved a mitt at the window, trying to think what she'd like.

"Sun catchers," Ike said. Simon looked at him gratefully. Ike snapped another flash picture of Ammy with his new digital camera, a Christmas present. He'd been taking pictures of her from every angle, while she ignored him.

Ammy stared through the frost-etched glass at the dinosaur models and microscope kits as if they were so many dead flies. Then she turned slowly on one heel and looked up and down the street at the rows of one- and two-storey buildings. "So this is your downtown."

"Not all of it." Simon pointed west. "There's Dunning Street and Wallace Street, that way. And there's three blocks of King Street," he pointed south, "all the way to the town hall —"

"Where," Ike finished, "everybody will be tomorrow night for Dunstone's Night of Magic."

"New Year's Eve street party," Simon explained. "Celeste will be there selling stuff, but we can just hang out." He watched her face hopefully.

"How come you call our grandmother by her first name? I've always wondered." It was her longest speech yet. Maybe she was loosening up.

"She likes it. Says it makes her feel less prehistoric. You should — "

"It's weird." Ammy slouched on along the street. The streetlights came on and a few snowflakes slid down through the cones of light. She rounded the corner onto King Street with Simon and Ike trailing her by several glum paces. Ike put his camera back into its case.

Two stores short of the town hall square was Helen's Travel. It was closed. Ammy looked into that window and stopped. And stared.

Simon couldn't see anything there worth staring at. A poster advertised vacations in the Bahamas, with palm trees and sand. Another poster showed mountains and llamas and people wearing those pointy knitted hats that you saw all over now.

Ammy thumped her forehead on the window. She kept it up, slowly, *bonk, bonk, bonk*. Ike stepped away from her. Simon pulled at her arm. "Ammy!"

She stopped thumping and looked at him. Her eyes were switched on, bright blue. "I should be there!"

"In the Bahamas? But —"

"No! In Peru!"

"Oh, I get it." Now he was sorry he'd wished her abducted by aliens. "Your parents. Of course." He caught Ike's eye, and they nodded at each other. They'd seen this news story the other day where an American businessman in Colombia had been kidnapped and held to ransom, and later returned to his family in six separate packages.

Now Ammy was only resting her forehead on the window. Simon tried patting her arm. She pushed him off. "I was so *happy* when they told me they were going to Peru to build a water treatment plant! Here was my chance to see the world. The Amazon! Jungles! Mountains!"

"The Amazon is in Brazil," Ike murmured.

Simon was confused. "What about the kidnappers?"

"Who said anything about kidnappers?" Ammy pushed away from the window.

"But isn't that what's worrying you?"

She frowned at him. "I'm not worried."

"About your parents?"

"They're perfectly safe!"

"Then what —"

"They *dumped* me!" She waved her arms. "Don't you get it? I've never been anywhere! This was my chance and they smashed it. I *love* mountains!"

"But you have mountains in British Columbia," Ike pointed out. "Quite a lot of them."

"These would've been new mountains. Foreign ones."

"Well, you're someplace new now." Simon pointed around at the street, the sky, everything. "You've never been here before."

"Oh, please! Dunstone? There's nothing here!" She started along the street again, only now she was stomping, not slouching.

Simon stomped after her. He was bigger and heavier than she was, and his pile-lined rubber galoshes stomped just as well as her Doc Martens. *So why don't you go back to Vancouver?* That's what he wanted to say. But Celeste had given him a mission.

"There's lots here if you'd only look!"

"Yeah, like what?"

"Well, like … like that." He pointed upward. "That" was the town hall, with its tower. It was the tallest building in town, if you didn't count the

Anglican and Catholic churches, which had spires, and the feed mill silo. The Welsh stonemasons who built the town hall 125 years ago hadn't been able to resist carving dragons, winged and coiling, all along the parapet at the top. The dragons, now locally famous, were floodlit in red and green for Christmas.

Ammy peered upward. "Can we go up there?" For the first time, she sounded interested.

"I'm pretty sure not," Simon said.

"Huh." She scuffed on. "What else?"

"Well, there's Founders Tower out on the edge of town, it's a kind of scenic lookout. And, um…" He groped for local excitement. She probably wouldn't think the curling rink was exciting. Beyond those three things, there was only…

"There's the gorge." Ike made a snaking motion with his hand. "It goes right through town. People come from all over for the rafting and the climbing. And the caves."

"Caves?" That perked her up.

"Yep, caves. And if you like mountains, well, the gorge is just like a row of mountains, right? Only, it's upside down." Ike sketched a *V* shape in the air.

"And inside out," Simon added.

"Inside-out upside-down mountains." Ammy almost let loose a grin, then. Almost. "Caves, huh? I bet if I said 'Let's go explore,' you'd say 'No!'"

"It's winter, Ammy," Simon said patiently. "Nobody goes in the gorge in winter."

"Amelia."

"A what?"

"Amelia. It's my name."

"But —"

"Ammy is an idiotic name." She jutted her chin. "It's a baby name. I don't know why I ever put up with it."

"I always kind of liked it, along with our last name. Ammy Hammer."

"Ammy Hammer." Ike laughed. "It's got a ring to it. Ammy Hammer!"

Simon joined in happily. "Ammy Hammer, Ammy Hammer!"

"Ammy Hammer, Ammy Ham—"

Ammy let out a yell and tackled Ike, and next moment they were rolling around in the snow piled at the edge of the street. Ammy was shrieking "It's Amelia! Say it! Say it!" and Ike was squealing and laughing.

Simon stood back out of range. This was more like it! At last Ike gasped, "It's Amelia!" and she let him up. They struggled upright, holding onto each other, and Simon brushed the snow and slush off their backs.

"All right!" Ammy ran her hands through her gelled hair, making it stick out in all directions. She grinned at Simon and poked Ike on the arm. "Let's go see this famous gorge of yours."

§

They walked past the new mall to Riverside Drive, left behind the fluorescent store lights and many-coloured Christmas lights, and kept on going through the bright circles under the streetlights and the dim stretches between them. They were alone. Nobody else was crazy enough to go walking in the cold and the dark on a December Sunday at dinnertime.

To their left, on the far side of the road, rose a snowy hillside patched black with pine trees. To their right was a waist-high stone wall, and on the other side of it some leafless bushes. Beyond that lay an abyss.

"Here's a good place." Simon stopped where the wall curved away from the road and back to enclose a semicircle of snowy asphalt. "Great view from here."

"What view?" Ammy leaned over the wall. Simon leaned over beside her and Ike straddled the wall on her other side.

"By daylight it's a great view," Simon explained.

A streetlight behind them struck gleams off the opposite lip of the abyss but cast the lower regions into blackness. Twisted sheets of ice draped the sides of the gorge and filled the bottom, visible only because they were so white. The only sound was the whine and rattle of wind in bare twigs.

Ammy stuck her hands into her armpits and stamped her feet. *Half frozen, and no wonder, dressed like that!* Simon resisted the urge to smack his mitts together. He hooked his thumbs casually in his pockets. "Had enough?"

"N-no. Wh-where are the caves?"

He wondered if she was putting him on. He never found out.

Ike yelped, "What's that?" and jumped down from the wall. Something was happening on the other side of the gorge, right across from them, about halfway down. Light streamed from a gap in the cliffside. Light of a sharp, electric blue.

And then the blue light flickered as something moved in front of it. Something came out of the gap and stood there outlined in brilliant streamers.

Simon shielded his eyes against the glare. He heard Ammy gasp.

CHAPTER TWO
SOMETHING LOST, SOMETHING FOUND

The gorge was dark again. Amelia pulled in one long breath — *Well, I wanted something exciting to happen* — then pushed it out again. *And something did happen.*

But what?

"My head hurts." She closed her eyes and rubbed them. Glowing blue splotches writhed and leaped across the blackness behind her eyelids.

"What was that?" asked Simon, to her right.

"Power lines?" That was Ike, to her left. "Maybe a transformer blew."

"In the gorge?"

"Seems funny, doesn't it? I'll ask my dad when I get home." Ike's voice was suddenly close to her ear. "My dad's the editor of the *Dunstone Independent*. Anything happens, he gets to know about it. Um, Ammy?"

She uncovered her eyes. "Amelia."

"Right. You okay?"

"No." Her head still hurt. And she was freezing. Her hands and ears ached with cold. She wished she had her Peruvian hat. "What happened just then?"

"There was this blue flash down in the gorge," Simon began.

"More like a flare," Ike said. "It got bright slowly, then it was really bright, then it sort of faded." He looked over the wall. "I think."

"I remember the light," Amelia said. "I've got this feeling there was something more. Like, something else happened that I can't remember."

"Aha!" Ike straightened up so fast he nearly left the ground. "Then we know what this is! It's an alien visitation!"

"Ike, not now, okay?" Simon sounded tired.

"But it's obvious! Here's Ammy, with half her brain sucked out —"

"Speak for yourself! My brain's all there."

"If it wasn't, you wouldn't know, would you?"

"I need to move," she said. "I'm turning into a block of ice."

They started back along Riverside Drive, with Amelia in the lead. Two steps, and the toe of her boot sent something bouncing along the ice-crusted sidewalk. It winked at her, one red gleam, as it flew. She nabbed it in midstride and stopped under the next streetlight to look at it.

Her first thought was that she held a lump of glass. A shiny pebble, heavy, dark, with a fiery spark at its heart. Then she rolled it over and saw the metal band.

"It's a ring!" Ike reached for it, but Amelia pulled her hand back.

"Somebody must've dropped it." She tucked it into her jacket pocket.

"You should put a notice in the *Independent*, in the lost and found column," Ike said. "It could be valuable. Maybe you'll get a big reward. Which you could share with us."

"Yeah, likely."

They walked on, passed the new mall with its wall of coldly lit windows, turned the bend onto King Street, passed stores in old brick buildings twinkling with coloured lights. There were more people here, more cars passing. Amelia felt safer.

Safer? Why shouldn't I feel safe?

Funny how tacky those lights look when Christmas is over, she thought, as they stopped at the corner of King and Peel and waited for a couple of pickup trucks to rumble past. And the red and green floodlights that splashed down the building fronts from the eaves were just plain ugly. What was worse, you couldn't see past them when you looked up. They made a ceiling of light. Anything could be up on those roofs, looking down, and you'd never know.

Peering upward under her hand, she made a sound. Simon pulled at her wrist. "What?"

"I saw something up there." She pointed at the roofline above Smith Hardware. "On the roof. Just a … a sort of flicker behind the lights."

Both boys squinted upward. "Can't see a thing with all that glare," Simon said.

"'Course, that doesn't mean there's nothing there," Ike said. "There could be. Easily." He looked at Amelia and his eyes brightened. "We're being followed!"

"Don't *say* that!" She darted across the street. Moving felt safer than standing still. It was like a hole had opened in the sky above her head, and if she moved fast she could get out from under it.

Only the hole's inside my head, not above it. In my memory. Something I've forgotten. Something about that blue light. And now all of a sudden I have this ring, as if it dropped out of that hole.

Amelia, chill!

She kicked a chunk of ice along the sidewalk. Ike fielded it with his boot and kicked it onward, and Simon jumped after it, and soon they were running and laughing and jostling for control of the ice chunk. They kept that up until they reached the town hall square. By then Amelia was starting to feel as if things were normal again.

Music tinkled at them as they trotted into the square. More people were here, mostly parents and young kids, skating on a rink in the middle of the square. The sound system was playing the Skater's Waltz. Amelia dropped onto a concrete bench and watched the skaters whiz and wobble past.

"You skate?" Simon asked.

"No. You?"

"A bit."

"Huh!" Ike snickered. "Simon's hopeless on skates. I'm good, though." He uncased his camera and walked over to the edge of the rink.

"Is he always like that?" she asked Simon.

"Yup, pretty much. He's, um…" Simon thought about it. "Playful."

She looked up at the town hall tower, with its carved parapet and red and green lights. You'd think they'd try different colours, like purple, or turquoise, or…

"Hey. I thought you said people can't go up there."

"I don't think they can. Why?"

"Oh … it's nothing." Her hands were shaking. She hid them in a fold of her scarf. "I saw something up there again, that's all. Above the lights. A — a face. A strange face." She heard the quaver in her voice and was angry with herself. "No, don't bother looking, it's gone."

"Somebody fixing the lights, maybe."

"Yeah, probably." Weird face, though, in that half-second. Too long, shaped wrong, you'd almost think it was one of those carvings, only it moved, and it looked right at her, and...

I must be really, really tired.

"Um, there's a coffee shop." Simon pointed across the square. "D'you want —"

"No! I'm perfectly fine."

He looked at her hands wrapped in her scarf, then took off his mitts and held them out.

"I said I'm fine!"

"You sure?"

"Yes!"

"Okay." He put his mitts back on.

Ike plopped down on the bench beside her. "Ammy, can I see that ring?"

She fished it out of her pocket and handed it over. "Be careful with it."

"You bet." He held it up sideways to his eye and looked at one of the streetlights through the curve of the stone, which rose a quarter-inch above the band. "Cool!"

"Let me see." Simon got it away from him and squinted through it with one eye. He panned the ring slowly across the square. "Neat! Everything's red. And it's all changed, all towers and mountains and things."

"Just as I suspected!" Ike hissed. "It's an alien artifact!"

Spare me! Amelia was suddenly too angry to be scared. That felt good. She gazed up at the black sky. "Please tell me, why, oh why am I hanging out with two geeky little boys?"

"Little?" Simon threw the ring into her hand. He looked as close to mad as she'd ever seen him. "I'm bigger than you!"

"Yes, but it's not size that counts, is it?"

"I'm older than you, too."

"Two months! Big deal!"

"Yeah, and look at you trying to look like a teenager! You —" He bit off whatever he'd been about to say and stared straight ahead. She'd swear he was counting to ten. Ike had scuttled away to the edge of the rink again.

"You see, Simon," she said in her kindest, most adult voice, "in the last two years I've matured, while you —" She looked him over, an outsized kid in parka and mittens and sensible boots, with his hair falling into his eyes. "I bet you still play with Lego."

"I do not!"

"Bet you do! Ha! You're turning red!"

He got up and stamped away a dozen steps, then stamped back. "Let's go home."

"Go home without me." She waved an airy hand.

"No. I promised Celeste. I'll stick with you if it kills me."

§

"Why can't she make her own supper?" Simon spread mustard on one half of a whole-wheat kaiser roll, lined it with lettuce, added a slice of tomato, and centred a piece of salami on it.

"Because she's far from home and tired and lonely. And she'll be getting hungry about now," Celeste said. "She didn't eat a crumb when I took her to lunch in Toronto. Nerves." She was sitting at the kitchen table wearing her black Indian caftan with the little mirrors bordered in silver embroidery, her long grey hair in a single braid. She nursed a cup of chai and watched him make his supper. Celeste never cooked, but she made sure he ate.

Simon cut cheese slices and slapped them down on the salami. "I still don't get why she has to stay with us. Wouldn't it be better for her to stay with that friend of hers in Vancouver?"

"Not while she's got us. It wouldn't be right. Family is family."

"Tell *her* that. I don't know what's the matter with her." He slashed another kaiser roll in half and stabbed his knife into the mustard jar. "She hates Dunstone. She hates me!"

"She doesn't hate you at all. She's just at a funny age. Probably isn't sure who or what she is, half the time."

"I'm the same age and I'm not like that!" He hacked at the block of cheese.

"Everyone's different." She tapped him on the wrist. "Go easy on her, okay?"

"*Me* go easy on *her*?"

Before he knew it his sandwich was ready, and so was Ammy's. He glanced at Celeste. "Will you call her?"

"No, you call her. Better yet, take it to her."

"But she —"

"*Simon.*"

He knew that tone of voice. While Celeste poured out a glass of milk, he cut one sandwich in half and put it on a plate. Then he carried the glass and plate out of the kitchen and along the hall to Ammy's room.

The door was closed. He knocked. "Ammy? It's me. You want a sandwich?" He hoped she would say no, or, better yet, throw a shoe or something at the door, so he could go away and say he'd done his best.

No such luck.

Chapter Three
The Ruby Ring

As soon as they got back to the apartment, Amelia went to her room and unpacked. As she shoved sweaters into drawers and lined up CDs on her desk, she thought about what to do.

It ain't over till it's over, she thought. That was one of her dad's favourite sayings. *Stick to it, girl* — that was something her mother liked to tell her.

Okay, I'll stick to it. I won't give up yet.

Her laptop was almost the first thing she'd unpacked. She sat down cross-legged on the bed, pulled the laptop close, and opened her mail. Nothing from her parents yet, but they'd given her the email address where they could be reached, once they got to their destination. She addressed a new message.

Dear Mom and Dad, I hope you get to Huaculamba soon so you can read this. Remember how you said you didn't want my education interrupted? Well, I have seen the school here and it is tiny! You probably didn't know that when you sent me here. So I am sure I can get just as good an education in Peru. I can bring textbooks and take online classes. Please let me know as soon as possible when I can come. Love, Ammy.

Then she backspaced over *Ammy* and typed in *AMELIA*, all in capitals. Her mother remembered to call her that now, most of the time, but her father still insisted on calling her Ammy. Usually Ammy the Something. Ammy the Great. Ammy the Terrible. Ammy the Barbarian, that was his latest.

"I am not a barbarian!" She scowled hideously at the computer screen and attacked the keys again. *btw, don't get kidnapped or anything and be careful driving on the mountain roads. And please write back soon!! I miss you!!! Lots of love, AMELIA.*

She clicked "Send," then started a new message.

Hi Silken! So here I am in an apartment in downtown Dunstone, Ontario. All my worst fears have come true. This place is dire. Luckily I won't be here long, I'll be in Peru soon if I can get my parents to see reason.

The one cool thing is our apartment building. It's old and only three floors high, with stores and a bank and a newspaper office on the ground floor and apartments on the top two floors. But nobody lives on the top floor right now, because people keep leaving Dunstone instead of coming here (big surprise) so Granny uses one of the top apartments for storage.

She stopped, deleted *Granny*, and typed in *Grandmother*.

So, what's cool, you ask? For one thing, my grandmother owns the building. It even has our name in a stone block over the front door. The Hammer Block, 1922. Also, it has these black iron fire escapes down the sides, just like Audrey Hepburn's building in that movie, Breakfast at Tiffany's, remember? And it has a marble lobby and this really slow, creaky brass elevator, like a cage with a criss-cross gate that you pull across.

The reason Grandmother needs all that storage is she has this store on the ground floor. It's called

Boomer Heaven. She says it's a pun on her name, Celeste. (Celestial, get it?) It has all kinds of real sixties and seventies junk. She's really retro herself, she wears these little gold-rimmed glasses like John Lennon's.

But guess what! Something weird happened right away. I was out walking with my cousin Simon, and there was this blue flash, and I

"And I what?" she said aloud. She shook her head, typed in *found*, then slipped her hand under the pillow for the ring.

What beautiful colour, now that she could see it. In this light the stone gleamed richly red. It was about half an inch across and smooth, not faceted. All the same, it looked precious. Could it be a ruby?

It was scratched, though. Too bad. She brought it close to her eyes. Wait a minute, these weren't random scratches. This was a picture. Or a logo. An oval — she closed one eye — no, an almond shape, with a line across the narrow part, like a cat's eye. At each pointed end a thin crescent, like a moon or a claw, continued the line of the eye, curving down and under on the left and up and over on the right.

Oddly enough, the setting and the band were plain and dull and looked like they'd been carved out of some brown old bone. Or maybe ivory, although ivory was illegal, she thought. She slid the ring onto the middle finger of her right hand, where it swung loose. Made for a man, then. A man with very thick fingers.

She wondered if he was sorry to lose it. "Well, too bad," she said crossly — crossly because she felt she was doing something wrong, somehow, and didn't like the feeling. "Finders keepers, losers weepers."

She held the ring to her eye and looked up at the overhead light through the curve of the stone. Inside there were branching lines that turned everything strange. She turned the ring to and fro and the square light shade forked like coral in a crimson sea.

She panned it across the room. The closet door and the dresser with its mirror and the open suitcase on it, clothes spilling, turned into a fantastic mountain landscape, volcanic, lava-draped, pocked with caves and crowned with spires. All ruby-coloured, alive, changing. You could almost see people at the cave mouths. Strange, long faces looking out.

She lowered the ring. Now, that was funny. Just for a second she was back in the town hall square, looking up at the tower. That glimpse of face had been just like... *Funny.*

Amelia put the ring to her eye again and scanned it slowly across the room. Ridges, peaks, deep ravines. Shapes raced across the mountainside, leaped into the air as the ring moved. Vanished in explosions of ruby light, like flame.

Wow, this was so —

A face that was all jaws swooped at her out of a blaze of red fire. She dropped the ring with a gasp, then grabbed it and shoved it under her pillow. Enough of that kid stuff!

The laptop went into screensaver mode. She revived it. *Silken, did you ever think you might be going crazy? If you ever did I wish you would tell me. I don't want to be the only one.*

A knock on the door. "Ammy? It's me. You want a sandwich?"

She was tempted to say no, except she was really hungry. And sooner or later she would have to speak to Simon again. *Poor Simon,* she thought. *Maybe I haven't been really ... I guess I ought to ... The adult thing would be...*

To apologize. She hated apologizing.

"Just a sec!" She typed *gtg. l8r. amelia,* clicked "Send," and shut down the laptop. When she opened the door a minute later he was still there, plate in one hand, glass of milk in the other. A wonderful smell came from the kitchen.

Simon held out the plate and glass. Amelia took them. "Thanks," she said. As he turned away she cleared her throat. "Um, and back in the square. When I called you a geeky little boy. That was ... I mean ... I'm sorry."

He gazed at the doorframe beside her head, then at her, as if he wasn't sure exactly what he'd heard. "Huh." Then he smiled. "Well, that's —"

"I mean, it may be true, but that's no excuse. I shouldn't have said it."

Simon didn't look as pleased as she thought he should have, but Amelia felt much better. She carried the glass and plate along the hallway to the kitchen. Grandmother was sitting at the table, sipping from a steaming cup. A platter of chocolate chip cookies sat in front of her.

"Oh, you baked. That's nice," Amelia said, politely. They did smell good.

"No, Schnarr's Bakery baked. Have some. *After* your sandwich."

Amelia set down her plate, slid into a chair across from Simon, and started eating. The moment her teeth sank into the sharp cheddar she realized she was famished. By the time the second half of the sandwich and most of the milk were gone, she was ready to look around and notice things outside herself.

The fridge bristled with sticky notes scribbled over with phone numbers and cryptic messages. "Velma S has stovepipes, gd cond." "Heart-shape rose-col glasses, yes!!"

In among the notes were photos held on with advertising magnets. Most of them were photos of her and Simon. There was Amelia — no, it was Ammy then —

in that dorky ponytail, hands on hips, putting on attitude for the camera. An even younger Ammy showing off a gap in her front teeth. Ammy on a tricycle, zooming past the camera, out of focus. Ammys of all sizes, back to the year she was born. It was embarrassing.

Photos of Simon, too, from this Christmas back to practically the day of his birth. In most of them, no matter what age, he wore the same patient expression. As if he was waiting for life to make sense. Only the earliest ones showed him with his parents, who were killed in a car accident when he was still a baby. Simon's father looked a lot like Amelia's, which wasn't surprising, since they were brothers. She wondered if it hurt Simon to look at those pictures. Could you could miss someone you'd never known? She hoped not.

She reached for a cookie. "Grandmother, if I got a picture of me with my hair like this, would you put it on the fridge?"

"Front and centre!"

Maybe it wouldn't be so dire after all, living here.

The cookies were awfully good. The three of them finished off the platter in the living room while watching *The Wizard of Oz* on TV. Later, Amelia wasn't sure what was to blame for the dream — the movie, all those cookies, or the ruby ring.

§

She dreamed, and knew she was dreaming. She was soaring in an ocean of sky. Far below lay a landscape of ruby-coloured pinnacles and deep black canyons steaming under a crimson sun.

She'd dreamed of flying before, but this was better. This was freedom! Nothing could scare her now, nothing could catch her. She wheeled and circled till her head spun. She soared towards the sun till her eyes were dazzled. Then dived at the ground, faster, faster, nearer.... Banked at the last possible moment. The world turned sideways; the pinnacles tilted and sank.

And then she saw that the land was not empty. Shapes were leaping from the ruby spires and arrowing towards her. She whirled in mid-air and flew, flew for her life, but something screamed in triumph right behind her and something sharp closed on her heel.

Amelia jerked awake and for a moment thought she was still dreaming. She wasn't in her bed. She was sitting on something hard in a dusty-smelling darkness. No, not darkness — solid blackness, with no vague window shapes in it. No hint of light anywhere. Sitting on ... it felt like wood, rough and grimy. And leaning against a ... it felt like a wooden wall.

Her hands groped out and felt wood on both sides, close. Too close. Like a coffin.

I've been buried alive!

CHAPTER FOUR
UP ON THE ROOF

Amelia's breath came quick and shallow. Her head started to buzz. *Don't panic!* snapped a sensible voice in the back of her head. Not a coffin, that's silly. You lie down in a coffin, you don't sit up.

A cellar, then. A sealed room in a cellar. That was almost as bad.

No, not a cellar. She sniffed. The smell was wrong. This place smelled of dust and old dry wood, not stone or cement or — oh, horror — earth.

So she was shut in somewhere, but not in a cellar. Where, then?

Don't just sit there, nagged the sensible voice. *Move! Find clues!*

She caught her breath with a gulp. The voice had arrived in her head about a year ago, when life had started to get so complicated. She wasn't sure what it meant. Crazy people heard voices. Only, the advice this voice urged on her was always sensible. Amelia had a suspicion it might even be her own voice, speaking up out of the chaos. If that was so, she was saner than she knew. Maybe there was hope after all.

Clues. Okay. Her heart quieted. But what clues? She couldn't even see!

She could feel, though. The wood against her shoulder was cold. A thin stream of freezing air needled at her hands. Close to the outdoors, then, she thought, and felt proud of the deduction. It showed she was using her head.

She moved her feet — they were bare — and traced a rounded edge with a drop below it. Felt downward: found more wood. A step. So this was a stairwell. But it wasn't the stairs she'd seen in the apartment building, because those were sheathed in marble.

How, she wondered, *did I get here — wherever this is — in my pyjamas and dressing gown?* It seemed she'd got up out of bed and put on her dressing gown and tied the sash, all in a sound sleep, before wandering away into the night. That was more bizarre than anything.

Where now? Down the stairs or up? A little more groping around showed that there was no more up. This was the top of the stairs. And the thing she was sitting against was a door, with a round metal handle and a metal bolt the length of her hand. A door! A way out! Yes!

She jumped up and raised her hand to the bolt. And froze there, hand hovering. The bolt creaked in its socket. She laid a hand softly on the door and it shifted under her fingers, as if the wood was breathing. Or bending, ever so slightly, inward.

Somebody was leaning on the other side of the wooden panel. Somebody large and heavy. Who was trying his best to be silent, which meant he knew she was here. Who was patiently waiting for her to slide the bolt and open the door.

Her thoughts flew to the ring she'd found, sized for a big man. Could he have traced her here? Was he here after his property? Was he furious?

Amelia eased backward down the stairs, one hand splayed on each side wall. She kept her face toward the unseen door. No way she was going to turn her back on it.

One slow downward step, then another.

And then another door crashed open below and a dazzling light blinded her.

§

"Wow!" Simon shook his head in admiration. "I don't think I ever saw anybody jump that high from a standing start before."

Ammy didn't seem to think it was funny. "You could've called out! Or knocked." She slumped against the wall and oozed down it until she was sitting on a step. "'Stead of just busting in like that. I could have broken my neck!"

"Well, you didn't. What are you doing here, anyway? It's two-thirty in the morning!"

She mumbled. Sounded like "… sleepwalking …"

"You're kidding! What's it like?"

"How should I know? I was in bed and then I was here. I've never done it before in my life!" She rubbed her eyes. "Where's here?"

"The stairs to the roof, what did you think?"

"I didn't think, I was asleep — remember? How'd you know I was here?"

"I heard you go out and it seemed weird, so I went looking for you." He jingled the keys in his dressing gown pocket. "You didn't leave the building — I could tell by the way the doors were locked — and you weren't in the basement, or in Celeste's storage room, so this was the only other place you could be."

"And you came looking … why?"

"Curious." And worried too, he would have added, if she'd been a bit friendlier.

Ammy pointed a trembling finger at the door to the roof. "Somebody's behind that door."

"Up there?" Simon shook his head. "Can't be. There's just the roof up there. This is the only way up. And" — he reached up past her and felt the bolt — "it's still locked."

"They could've got up by the fire escape."

"Uh-uh. The bottoms of the ladders are twelve feet off the ground."

"Then what the heck good are they?"

Patience, he told himself. "You get down to the lowest landing and then there's no more stairs — there's a ladder you unhook and it slides down. Pretty clever, actually. They're for escaping from fires, just like the name says. You're not supposed to use them to climb up."

"Then how did that person get on the roof?"

"Ammy, there's nobody on the roof."

"There is!"

No point in arguing, he decided. "We'll take a look."

"All right!" She stood up and tightened the sash of her dressing gown.

The sensible thing, of course, would have been to go back downstairs and wake Celeste. If he'd been by himself and thought somebody was on the roof who shouldn't be, that's what he'd have done. But here was Ammy, with a glint in her eye that didn't look sensible. And it was the dead of night, and the whole town was asleep except them, and something strange was in the air.

Besides, that crack about "geeky little boys" from this afternoon still rankled, despite — or maybe because of — Ammy's backhanded apology. Of course, he had nothing to prove. But he was glad he was wearing the grown-up-looking navy blue robe Celeste had given him for Christmas, instead of his old one with the *Star Trek* motif.

We'll be back inside in no time, Simon promised himself. Ammy had on a thin, silky, red Chinese-patterned robe. She wouldn't last ten seconds.

And her feet were bare. That wouldn't do. "Where are your slippers?"

"Slippers?" She grimaced. "I don't own any. Slippers are dorky."

Trust Ammy. He sat down and pulled off his slippers. "Put these on."

"But you —"

"I have socks on too, see?" He stuck out a foot to show her.

"You wear slippers *and* socks?"

"With our cold floors? Sure."

She made a sound that was not quite a snicker, but consented to put on the slippers. They were too big, so he gave her his socks — tight-knit, waterproof, real wool socks — and he wore the slippers. Then he stood up, pulled back the bolt, and swung the door wide. Icy air flooded in.

Nothing and nobody was out there. He stepped gingerly out on the squeaking crust of snow. Ammy stepped out after him, her hands deep inside her silken sleeves. Waves of snow blew over the surface, filling in whatever footprints there might have been.

"Just a quick look round." Simon led the way toward the waist-high parapet that edged the roof. Breath clouds whipped away from his mouth.

The top of the stairs was covered with a little hut. The roof was flat and, aside from the hut and six brick chimneys sticking up, it was bare. If they hadn't been freezing to death they might have admired the view of Dunstone's lights below and the sharp stars above.

Simon hunched his shoulders to his ears. "S-seen enough?"

"Y-y-yeah."

They scurried back. Just short of the hut, Ammy stopped. "What's that up there?"

A black shape sat on top of the hut. "Pile of sacks? Boxes?"

"But it…"

It moved. Uncurled and stretched. Stood up.

Simon's mouth dropped open. It — she — was a woman, or maybe a girl, by the shape. That was about all you could see in the starlight. What kept Simon's mouth hanging open was that … it was hard to tell in this light, but it looked like she was dressed in nothing but her long, tangled hair.

CHAPTER FIVE
GIRL BY STARLIGHT

For a couple of heartbeats, the only sound was the hiss of snow blowing over the frozen crust. Then Amelia leaned to Simon's ear. "Careful!" she whispered. "Don't scare her."

"Wha...?" He was staring at the girl like his eyelids were velcroed open. Suddenly they squeezed shut. "*What?*"

"I said, don't scare her."

"She doesn't look scared."

That was true. The girl stood straight, hands at sides. Staring back at them, Amelia thought, although that was hard to tell. She could have been standing on a beach in July. Here, in this weather, in nothing but her skin. Bonkers. Totally.

Simon grabbed her arm. "Come on! We've got to tell Celeste."

"No! We've got to get her inside first. She'll freeze if we leave her there!" She pulled him close and muttered, "Or maybe she'll...." She tilted her head at the parapet. "And then how will we feel?"

His eyes widened. "You think that's why she came up here?"

"Who knows? Give me your dressing gown. Yours is longer."

"Why?" His eyes darted up at the girl and snapped down again. "Oh, right." He dug the ring of keys out of his pocket and pulled at his sash, but not fast enough. Amelia peeled the robe off him and dumped it onto the roof of the hut. "Go ahead, put that on!"

The girl just nudged the robe with her foot. It was a long foot with sharp toenails, crusted with snow.

"Let's g-get Celeste." Simon flailed his arms around his sides. "Can't you s-see there's something wrong with her?"

"Sure I can. But...." Amelia sank her hands into her pockets. Her fingers closed on the ruby ring. How did that get there? And, funny — instead of being cold it was warm. Holding it was like holding somebody's hand. It helped. She squeezed, then let it go.

"Help me get up there," she said. "And don't argue!"

It was only when Amelia was standing on the hut roof beside the girl that she felt afraid. Only then did she realize how tall the girl was — as tall as her dad, at least. The face staring down at her from its tangle of hair was only a shadow with two faint lights in it.

This is no time to get scared! She stooped for the robe and draped it over the girl's shoulders. Delicate, like cats' bones. The girl just stood there, as if she didn't know what clothes were for. Amelia pushed thin arms into sleeves, pulled the robe closed, and tied the sash.

"Come on, then. Come down where it's warm." The girl didn't move. Amelia tugged at her sleeve and pointed downward. "You'd like to be warm, yes? Warm?"

"Waaarm." A husky whisper.

"All right. I'm going down. Then you come too. Okay?"

She slithered off the roof, landed beside Simon, and brushed snow off her robe. "See? If I can do it, you can do it!" She waved encouragingly. "Don't be afraid, it's not far."

The girl stood still a moment, staring down at her. Then she took one step off the hut roof and dropped straight down. She landed as if she weighed next to nothing. Snow puffed up from under her feet and swirled around her. She laughed silently and put out a pointed pink tongue to catch the glittering motes.

Once she'd decided to move, it wasn't hard to guide her into the hut and down the stairs. Then Amelia had to lead her all the way along the corridor to the main stairs at the front of the building. Simon walked ahead. He kept taking nervous looks back over his shoulder.

He was two steps away from the stairs when the girl stopped short. "No," she said.

Ammy tugged gently at her arm. "Come on, it's okay. There's nothing to be scared of."

"No."

"Could be she wants to know where we're taking her." Simon came back from the stairs. "Maybe she's afraid we'll call the cops."

"Of course we won't! Why would we do that?"

"Because maybe she belongs in some *hospital.*" He stared hard and meaningfully at Amelia. "Maybe people are looking for her right now."

The tall girl gazed down at them, eyes moving from face to face as they spoke. She looked alert and interested and not crazy at all.

They could see her properly now, in the corridor light. She looked about fifteen, Amelia thought. Sixteen at most. But not like any sixteen-year-old she'd ever seen before.

Dark red hair sparked with gold fell below her hips. Her eyes were large and gold-green and tilted like a cat's. Her skin was so thin you could see blue veins at her temples and on her hands. You'd think a breeze would blow her away.

"We don't even know her name," Simon said.

"That's right!" Amelia faced the girl. She slapped Simon's shoulder. "He's Simon. *Simon*. And I" — she touched her chest — "I'm Amelia. *Amelia*."

The girl lifted a long hand and ran her fingers over the tips of Amelia's neon hair. Her lips parted. Was that a smile? The points of her white teeth gleamed.

"And you? What's your name?" Amelia touched the girl's arm. "Your *name*?"

The girl lifted her head. Her lips closed; her eyes darkened. The corridor chilled. Amelia stepped back.

"Ammy, I think we should talk." Simon tried to pull her towards the stairs. "Without her. With Celeste."

"But we can't leave her here by herself!" She yanked her arm free.

"Not to worry, we'll put her in here." He walked over to the nearest closed apartment door. A brass 3A was bolted to the panel below a glass peephole. "Celeste's storage room."

"It'll be locked."

"Not a problem." He swung the ring of keys on his finger.

Amelia was diverted. "What's that, every key you ever owned?"

"Celeste made me copies of all her keys, just in case. I always carry them." He flipped through the collection, chose one, and unlocked the door. He reached in and switched on the light, then waved the others in ahead of him.

The living room was crowded. A table with a sewing machine stood along one wall. Beside it ran a row of cardboard boxes stacked three and four high. A green sofa with stuffing sprouting from the arms faced the doorway, and a massive wooden cupboard filled one corner.

The girl immediately crossed to the window and tried to open it. "No!" Amelia dashed over. "Too cold!" She thought of the three-storey drop outside.

The girl ignored her. It was a double-hung window, the kind you slide up from the bottom. After a few seconds of pushing and shaking the frame, she discovered the latch at the top of the lower section. She twisted it, raised the window, and stuck her head and shoulders out. A fire escape landing was right outside. She closed the window without latching it. Amelia breathed again.

The girl looked the window up and down as if making sure the way it worked was fixed in her mind. She'd never seen that kind of window before, Amelia realized. And then: *She wants to be sure there's a way out.*

"Interesting," murmured Simon, close behind her. "Let's go."

They both turned, took a couple of steps, and lurched.

"Uh-oh!" Simon said.

The girl held them each by an arm. "No," she said.

"We're just going to get help." Amelia tried to pry the fingers off her arm. They looked like twigs but felt like steel.

Simon winced. "What did I tell you?"

"We won't do anything to hurt you. I promise!" Amelia tugged at the hand. Its strength frightened her.

The girl let them go so suddenly, Amelia staggered and Simon fell against the door. Then before they could move she was across the room. Up with the window, out on the fire escape. One bound and she was up on the iron railing.

Amelia started to climb out the window. Simon pulled her back.

"But she'll fall!"

"You go out there and she'll jump."

The girl stood easily on the railing, facing out. The wind had picked up. Her hair was a blizzard of red. Simon's heavy dressing gown flapped. *But she looks a lot steadier than me*, Amelia thought. Poised on her toes, like a bird about to take flight.

"Please…" Amelia quavered. "Please come down."

The girl glanced over her shoulder. "No tell."

"No, of course I won't tell."

The girl pivoted on one foot. The wind battered her. She swayed. Any second now…

She stabbed a finger at Simon. "He."

"He won't tell, either. I promise! Now, please, please..."

The girl looked straight into her eyes. Her stare was like two strong hands gripping Amelia's shoulders. "You promise."

"Yes, yes! I promise! I said I do! Believe me!"

Her eyes flicked at Simon, then back at Amelia. "He promise."

"Yes, he promises too. Simon? Say it!"

"Sure, I promise," said Simon from behind her head.

The girl held Amelia's eyes a moment longer. Then she jumped back down onto the fire escape, ducked through the window into the room, and gripped both their outstretched hands. "I hear you. I believe."

CHAPTER SIX
COUGAR ON A LEDGE

Before they left 3A, Ammy found a chipped china mug in the kitchen and showed the girl how to get a drink of water. Funny, Simon thought, that she had to be shown. And after that she kept turning the taps on and off. She seemed fascinated by the way the water flowed and stopped. Ammy had to show her how to turn the lights off, too.

"Well, you've really dropped us in it now," he said, when they were out in the corridor. "Now she'll be really upset when we tell Celeste."

"What? Wait a minute!" Ammy swung around to face him at the top of the stairs. "Of course we're not going to tell Grandmother!"

"But we have to!"

"We can't! We promised. And she said, *I believe.*"

"But it's like she forced us. That's not a real promise."

"Oh, no? Well, my promise was real and I thought yours was too." She jabbed a forefinger at his chest. "And if you break your promise, I won't ever forgive you!"

Simon had a painful vision of what it would be like to live for six months with an unforgiving Ammy.

"Besides, it'll only be for a day or two." She turned and headed down the stairs. "Until we figure out what to do."

"Just for a day, then."

"Or two."

They agreed on one thing, at least. The girl needed warmth, food, and proper clothes. The first two turned out to be Simon's job. Back in the apartment, he grabbed the extra blanket from the foot of his bed, detoured to the kitchen for an orange and a bag of mixed nuts, and slipped out again.

Upstairs he knocked softly on the door of 3A. There was no answer. He unlocked it, opened it about six inches, then bent down, set the blanket and food on the floor, and pushed them through the dark gap. A bony hand clamped on his wrist and he froze. Two glinting eyes stared into his. *Like she's scanning my ID.* Then she let go and the door closed.

§

Simon dreamed of an elderly gerbil straining to spin a giant exercise wheel. *Squeak, clatter, grind … squeak, clatter, grind*. The rhythmic creaking scattered the last of his sleep.

Yawning, he sat up. Felt around on the floor for his socks. No socks. Groped on the coverlet for his robe. No robe. *What the heck?*

Then he remembered.

On his way to the kitchen in pyjamas and a clean pair of socks, he thumped on Ammy's door. She groaned.

He was pouring orange juice into a glass when Ammy shambled in, still in her pyjamas and red silk dressing gown, and barefoot. Her red and yellow hair stuck out in all directions. She looked like a porcupine that had lost a paintball fight. He opened his mouth to tell her so, then got a good look at her face and closed his mouth. He reached for a second glass and poured.

"Well! Up at last!" came a voice behind them. Celeste stood in the doorway, trim and chipper in jeans and an Aran sweater, with her silver braid over one shoulder. "Shame on the pair of you! Nearly noon! And no wonder, romping around the building when you should be asleep."

Ammy clasped her juice glass in both hands. "You heard?"

"I'm not deaf yet." She laughed. "Don't look so guilty! I don't mind if you poke around in my storeroom, so long as you keep things in good order. I do plan to sell that stuff, someday."

"Uh, it was me up there too, Celeste."

"Well, don't make a habit of it. Not in the middle of the night, anyway. At your age you need your sleep. Agreed?"

"You bet."

"Of course, Grandmother."

Simon put down his glass. There was that rhythmic, creaky sound again. This time he knew what it was. "That's the elevator."

Celeste glanced upward. "Third trip this morning. I finally got Lillian Smyth to sell me the boxes from her attic. That woman hasn't thrown away a stitch in fifty years."

"It's going in 3A?"

"Where else?"

Ammy and Simon looked at each other. Then Ammy bolted out of the kitchen and up the stairs. Simon was so close behind he nearly stepped on her heels.

The door of 3A stood open. They found one man stacking cartons along a wall while a second man sprawled on the couch, feet stuck out in front. The girl crouched on top of the armoire, in the corner. Neither of the men paid her any attention.

The man on the couch was lighting a cigarette. The plastic lighter went *click*, *click*, and the flame flared, and the girl went as tense as a cougar on a ledge. It seemed to Simon that the shadows in that corner darkened and spread around her. He held his breath.

"And just where d'you think you are?"

Ammy jumped a mile. Celeste stood right behind them. She waved them aside and strode forward. "That!" She pointed. "Out the window!"

"Oh, but, please! She's —" Ammy began.

"Sh!" Simon had a glimmer of what was happening. What, but not how.

The man on the couch put on a martyred look, got up, opened the window, and flicked the cigarette out onto the fire escape.

"Cigarette smoke in my house!" Celeste said, as she signed the bill. "I ought to dock you for the stink. You're darn lucky I'm in a good mood." They clumped out. Fists on hips, Celeste looked around the room. The girl crouched, watching, still as stone.

"There now!" Celeste spun around. "Who's for brunch?"

"I..." Ammy kept looking at the girl on the armoire.

Simon tugged at her wrist. "Me. I'm starving."

"You're always starving." Celeste ruffled his hair. "Just this once, I'll put myself out. Neither of you looks like you'd know one end of an egg from the other."

As he left, Simon saw that the blanket still lay folded by the door. The nuts were gone, but the orange had only one bite out of it, right through the peel.

§

After brunch Celeste went down to Boomer Heaven. "Lots to do," she said. "Got to be ready for tonight!"

"What's tonight?" Ammy asked.

"Tonight's New Year's Eve, of course. Dunstone's Night of Magic! I have to get my sale goods organized. Which reminds me. You" — Celeste pointed at Ammy — "before you leave this house, are going to find yourself a pair of mitts in the front cupboard. And you're going to wear them."

"Mitts!" Ammy looked as if she'd been told to find a boa constrictor and wear it around her neck. "But I never wear mitts!"

"And why in Pete's name not?"

"They're so dorky! Nobody wears them!"

"You will, though. And you'll be happy not to freeze your fingers off. Make sure of it," Celeste said to Simon, tapping him on the shoulder.

§

After Celeste left, Ammy rushed upstairs, still in pyjamas and dressing gown, balancing a stack of juice boxes and a plate of buttered toast. Simon dressed and was about to follow her when the phone in the kitchen rang. It was Ike.

"Simon! Did you hear?"

"Hear what?"

"About the blue flare last night."

"No, what about it?"

"I asked my dad. He hadn't heard anything. So this morning I called the police and the hydro." His voice dropped. "It wasn't anything electrical!"

"So?"

"Well, what else could it be? Think!"

Simon leaned back against the kitchen counter, prepared to be patient. "Lightning?"

"We both know it didn't go like lightning. Remember the slow fade?"

"You have an idea?"

"Yep."

"A sane idea? Not like —"

"No, no, no, not like that time on the school roof."

"Well?"

"You'll see. Meet me at one-thirty on Deacon Street by the trail down to the river. You got a ski pole?"

"What would I be doing with a ski pole?"

"Okay, I'll see what I can find. You just bring Ammy."

"Ammy? Why?"

"Don't you get it? She found the ring, she had the blackout. She has to be the key to this whole thing!"

"What whole thing?"

"Just be there." Ike hung up.

CHAPTER SEVEN
REFUGEE

"Now, that's what I call hot!" Amelia smoothed bright red angora over the girl's shoulders and smiled at her in the bathroom mirror. It was the girl's own choice, that red sweater. A hopeful sign, Amelia thought. If you were really in a bad state of mind, bad enough to think of jumping off a building, you wouldn't wear red, would you? In fact, you probably wouldn't be interested in what colours you wore at all.

Amelia had also found jeans, socks, and sneakers in one of Celeste's boxes, and she'd lent some of her own underwear. The girl hadn't been sure what to do with it all, at first, but she caught on fast.

"Hot." The girl watched her reflection with narrowed eyes. "Before, you say cool."

"Hot is better than cool."

"Good. Then I am hot." She laughed. The laugh was low, husky. Rusty, like it hadn't had much practice.

"Where's she from?" said Simon from the doorway. "Have you found that out yet?"

"Sh!" Amelia backed him out of the bathroom. "You talk like she's deaf!"

"Well, if she doesn't understand —"

The girl looked at him over Amelia's head. "I understand. Much."

"She's picking up English like crazy. So watch what you say!"

"That's good." Simon stopped backing up and bobbed to see past Amelia. "Where are you from? Why are you hiding here?"

"Not hiding."

"Are you in trouble? We can help you get home, or somewhere safe."

"My home is far. I will go soon."

"Well, that's good to hear. What's your na—"

Amelia grabbed his arm with both hands and rushed him to the apartment door. She snatched his navy blue dressing gown off the couch in passing, pushed the robe into his arms and him into the corridor, then slammed the door behind them and leaned on it.

"What's the matter? I only asked her name."

"Well, don't! She hates that!"

"Why? Never mind. Come outside, we've got to talk."

"Give me a minute, I can't go out in my pyjamas."

After Amelia finished dressing she unplugged the radio from her room and carried it upstairs, where the girl was curled up on top of the armoire again. She plugged the radio into the wall and turned it on. Avril Lavigne was singing "Complicated." The girl uncurled straight up and stared. "There!" Amelia patted the radio. "That'll be company for you."

She zipped up her leather jacket on the way down the stairs. Because the thermometer said twenty below zero Celsius, she'd caved in and pulled on her only hat, the multicoloured woolen one, made by Peruvian villagers, that made her think of her parents. She coiled her red scarf (really long, and cool) several times around her neck.

Simon was waiting for her on the stairs. He already had his baggy old grey parka on, with the green plaid-lined hood. "I've been thinking about what happened this morning, with Celeste and those men," he said. "I can't figure it out."

"Mm ... well ... she was up above them, and that corner is kind of dark, and she kept really still. I bet I wouldn't have noticed her, if I hadn't known she was there."

"Celeste would've. Should've. She doesn't miss anything, usually."

"Well, she did this time. No big mystery."

"She creeps me out, that girl." Simon led the way down the stairs. "There's just something about her...." He gave himself a shake. "I mean, she acts like she never saw a water tap before, or an orange."

Or a radio, Amelia thought. *Or underwear.*

"It's other things, too. Like last night on the roof, her in her bare skin, and she didn't seem to notice the cold. That's totally weird."

"She's just different." *Not like anybody I ever met before.*

"I wonder if she's running from the police?" They reached the lobby and Simon stopped halfway out the door. "We could get in big trouble by helping her."

"She's not a criminal!" Amelia pushed at him and he stepped out into the wind and snow.

"So what's going on here?" Simon demanded. "Gang wars? Bikers? Foreign spies?"

"Maybe she's some kind of refugee. Or maybe a crazy boyfriend is after her."

"Great. Just great."

"And maybe she'd be killed if she went back where she came from, ever think of that? Anyway, we promised."

"I know, I know! It's just..." They walked past a storefront with a painted sign above the window that said "DUNSTONE INDEPENDENT — FOUNDED 1910." Next door to the newspaper office was Boomer

Heaven. Inside, through the window, they saw Celeste with a customer. Celeste was talking with her hands. The woman was laughing. Simon put his head down and walked faster. "I feel bad about not telling Celeste. It's like lying to her."

"I feel bad about that too. But it won't be for long."

"It better not be. Oh, here." He stopped and pulled a wad of black leather from his parka pocket. He held it out. She didn't take it.

"What's that, mitts? I don't wear mitts."

"Celeste says you do. You know what that means. Besides, they're not mitts, they're gloves."

He stood there in front of her, holding out the squashed handful, blocking the sidewalk. He looked more than usually solid. As if he was prepared to keep her there all day, if he had to. She sighed deeply, took the gloves, and pulled them on. They were thick black leather, worn to softness, and lined with fleece. Too big, but they felt amazing on her hands. "Yours?"

"Yeah. Used to be my dad's. I figured there was nothing else in the closet I could get you to wear."

"You got that right." She shoved her gloved hands in her pockets and walked on, head down. It was irritating to have to admit Simon could be smart about some things. "They're cool," she muttered. "Thanks."

"Just don't lose them." He pushed back a navy blue wool mitten to see his watch. "Still time to catch Ike before he goes off on his own."

"Go. I have to get back now." She looked back along King Street. You could just see the top of their building from here, jutting above the lower roofs. What would the girl be thinking, all alone? That she'd been abandoned?

"Ike says you should come too."

"Come where? Why?"

"He won't say, but I think I know. To the gorge. Where we saw that blue flare."

"Why would I want to?"

He shrugged. "You said you saw something. Something that we missed, I guess. Then you forgot it. Maybe going there will help you remember."

She thought back. Blue light, and something moving in front of it, and... *Do I really want to remember?* She caught her breath with a gasp and realized she hadn't been breathing at all.

A hand on her arm. "You okay?"

She shook it off. "Of course I'm okay! It's just — she'll worry."

"Since we found her last night," Simon said, walking beside her, "I've never seen her look worried. Not once."

Well, that was true.

"It won't kill her to be by herself an hour."

That was true too. She hoped.

CHAPTER EIGHT
THE SAPPHIRE DOOR

"A sane idea, I thought you said," Simon said to Ike as he leaned over the stone wall at the end of Deacon Street and squinted down. The sun was out now, and the gorge in its ice drapings and fresh snow was a blaze of reflected light. Nobody was in sight besides themselves. In any other season, this strip of parkland between the gorge and the back fences of people's houses would be busy with walkers. Now it was an arctic waste, snowy and deserted.

"Go down there?" Ammy leaned over beside Simon. "We'll kill ourselves!"

"It's totally safe, if you have the right equipment. Like mountain climbing. Take this." Ike put a ski pole in her hand and gave another one to Simon. "I'll use the hiking pole. There's an easy path to the bottom —"

"Yeah, straight down!" Ammy waved her pole in an arc.

"— and the cave itself shouldn't be hard to reach."

"You knew about this cave?" Ammy looked along the gorge, northeastward, towards the spot on the opposite cliff edge where they'd been standing last night.

"I'm pretty sure it's the one I picked out this morning, from the other side. C'mon." Ike climbed over the wall and started down a steep path cutting slantwise down the face of the cliff. With one hand he grabbed hold of the cedars that grew between the rocks, and with the other he jabbed the hiking pole into the ice.

Well, if Ike could do it.... Simon followed him. The veil of snow gave an extra slipperiness to the ribbons of ice that twined between the rocks and the tree roots.

"Ammy?" he called back. "You coming?"

"Yeah." She sounded breathless.

Simon nailed his attention to the next two feet of path. Ike's head bobbed in the edge of his vision below. From above and behind came sounds of irregular breathing, thrashing cedar boughs, and steel on ice.

"Halfway down!" Ike called. Another couple of yards, and Simon started to relax.

Then Ammy yelled, and the yell swept closer. "Ike!" Simon gasped. "Watch —"

Something hit him behind the knees.

Ten seconds later, Ike picked himself up and nodded up at the cliff. "There, we're down. Not the way I planned," he said, bending to pick up his hiking pole, "but it wasn't so bad."

Ammy struggled to her feet and rubbed her hip. She said nothing, which Simon thought was ominous.

"Next time you mention ski poles," Simon said, unfolding himself from the ground, "I'm going to go home and lock the door."

Ike uncased his digital camera and checked it over. "No harm done. Ammy? You okay?"

"No!"

"You look okay. Let's head on out."

Travelling along the flat rocks at the base of the cliff was easier than climbing down, Simon found. You slithered and slid and fell down a lot, but at least you couldn't fall far.

The climb to the cave turned out to be the easiest part of the expedition. The cave mouth and the rocks below it were sheltered by the overhanging top of the cliff and almost completely free of ice. The rough layers of stone and the scrubby cedars, deeply rooted among the rocks, gave plenty of handholds and footholds.

Ike was the first to climb level with the rock apron in front of the cave mouth. "Hey!" he yelled. "Something's been here! Look at the evidence!"

A minute of breathless scrambling, and the three of them stood together on the ledge in front of the cave, all crowded against the cliff so as not to mess up the evidence. The entrance to the cave was about three feet high and wider than it was tall.

"Funny kind of tracks," Simon said.

They were looking at a trail of scuffed footprints leading from the bare rock inside the cave and across the snowy ledge to the cliff, where it disappeared. One or two of the prints were clear. Somebody with long nails on his feet, Simon thought. His *bare* feet. An image flashed through Simon's brain: a man with huge bare feet and toes with long talons, like a gigantic lizard. A chill ran down his spine. He stared at Ike, and Ike stared back at him.

Ammy, who had been very quiet, ducked down and peered inside the cave. Then she dropped to hands and knees and crawled in.

"Don't mess anything up!" Ike called after her.

"Ike," Simon said, "it snowed this morning. These tracks, whatever they are, can't have anything to do with last night."

"I thought of that. They must be the second wave."

"Of?"

"Intelligent dinosaurs, obviously." Ike had his camera out and was taking pictures. "What else could have made those marks?"

Simon studied them. "So you're thinking..."

"UFO."

"You're serious?" With Ike, it was sometimes hard to be sure.

"I wasn't at first." Ike's freckles stood out sharply, the way they always did when he was scared. "I mean, I was, but not seriously. But now it all hangs together. Don't you think?" He clutched his camera. "The blue flare with no known cause. Ammy with half her brain sucked out. That alien artifact she found."

"What? Oh, that ring."

"And now this." Ike waved at the strange tracks. "If a gigantic lizard didn't walk there, what did?"

They studied the tracks. "Grizzly," Simon said, after a moment. "We looked them up last winter for that science project on habitats, remember? Their footprints have that kind of long, almost human shape."

"I *see*!" Ike beamed at him. "Only..." He frowned. "No good. No grizzlies around here. They're all out west."

"Look, if you can believe in gigantic lizards —"

Ike whooped. "I got it! Soccer shoes!"

"Sure, the cleats!" Simon laughed. "No, wait! Crampons. You know, you've seen the people who go climbing here. Crampons are those pointy steel things they strap to their boots."

"But those look like bare feet."

"Um … moccasins?"

"That would be it, then." Ike sighed. "I feel a lot better. Not that I really believed in the gigantic lizard theory."

"Right."

"Only, how come the trail starts in the cave?" Ike peered into the opening, where Ammy had disappeared. "Where'd our guy come from?"

Simon nodded at the cliff, where the tracks stopped. "You've got it the wrong way round. He must've climbed down from above, went in the cave, was in there while it snowed — which covered up his first tracks — came out, and climbed up again."

The pink was back in Ike's cheeks. "That makes sense. Sometimes your brain works pretty good, Hammer! All right, where's Ammy? I want to test that artifact."

"Ammy?" Simon bent to look into the cave. You couldn't see anything after the first couple of feet. "Ammy?"

No answer. He called again, louder. Nothing. "How deep is this thing?"

"Well, if aliens are using it as a rendezvous —"

"Ike!"

"No idea."

"Got a flashlight?"

"Sure." Ike rummaged in his parka and pulled out a key ring with a folding knife and a finger-sized flashlight on it. He detached the flashlight and gave it to Simon. "You lead."

§

The cave was deeper than it looked from the outside. Just when it started getting really dark and Amelia was thinking about crawling back out, a dim light appeared. Ice crunched and gleamed under her hands. Space opened above her. She stood up.

"Huh!" she said. The air whispered back at her. It sounded bigger than it was, too. But aside from that, it was a disappointment. No measureless caverns here, no bottomless pools. And no stalagmites or stalactites, unless you counted the icicles hanging from the ceiling.

Amelia stood on a rough, ice-slicked floor in a bottle of rock. It was about ten feet across at the bottom, narrowing to a jagged crack of brightness high above, where two rock faces leaned together.

That crack, she realized, as her eyes adjusted to the dimness, was the reason she could see at all. Up above in the park there must be a heap of rocks with a gap in the middle. That also explained the icicles and the ice on the floor.

It wasn't even a secret cave. People had been here before. They'd scratched initials and hearts and rude words into the rocks. Right in front of her, on a smooth

patch, someone had used thick purple marker to print:
"R U ANYONE YET?"

"Who knows?" Amelia said to the wall. Her voice
bounced back at her from all around. "Knows …
knows … no…"

An echo, in this little cave. Now, that was cool.

"I'm me!" she declared. "So there!"

"Me … there … me … air…" muttered the echoes.

Amelia laughed, and touched the wall with her
gloved hand, and turned to go.

Blue light tugged at the edge of her vision. She
swung around.

Down the rock face she'd just touched hung a
gauzy blue curtain. No, not gauze. It was light: blue
light, first pale and vague, then brighter, more definite.
Now it was a tall rectangle with an arched top. Its blue
was the rich colour of a clear evening sky the moment
before true night closes in. Or a sapphire with light
shining through it, which Amelia recognized because
her mother had a small one in a pendant.

She backed away until her head hit the slanting rock
on the other side of the cave. Her vision darkened.
Bright motes swarmed across the darkness.

When her sight cleared the blue rectangle looked
even more solid. Like you could actually touch it, if you
dared. Intertwining ridges, like the stems of ivy, covered
the surface. It could have been a door, only there was

no handle. Or a window, because it looked like a slab of glass, with the blue glow behind it, only you couldn't see through it.

"Hey, guys!" Amelia croaked.

In the time it took to draw another breath, the image changed again. The blue glow seeped away like water sinking into sand. Patches of dark rock seeped forward. Another breath and, whatever it was, it was gone.

Chapter Nine
Unbreakable

"Aha!" Ike said. "She remembers! It all comes back!"

Simon played the flashlight's thin beam over her face. She put up a hand to shield her eyes. She did look pretty stunned. "You all right, Ammy?"

"What can you remember?" Ike demanded.

"No. Yes. Nothing. I..." She closed her eyes. Then opened them. Speaking quietly and precisely she said, "I don't remember anything. From last night. I *saw* something. Now."

"Yes!" Ike punched the air. "Oh, wow! Listen to the echo!"

"It was blue. It was the same colour as that blue light last night. It was tall and like a door, with a curve on top. It was right *there*." She pointed at the cave wall. Ike stepped over and felt the wall.

"A door to another dimension!" He nudged Simon. "That would explain how the light got brighter and then faded. It was the door, opening and closing. That's perfect!"

"You're playing," Ammy said, still in that small, precise voice.

"Of course not!" Ike turned on his most endearing grin. "I'm totally serious."

"You're playing. I'm serious." She pulled off her gloves, stuffed them in her pockets, and swept her hands over the wall. "It was right here!" She slapped the rock. "I just touched it, like that, and there it was."

"Ammy, take it easy." Simon pulled her sleeve. "I think I know what you saw."

"I saw a *door*."

"Well, maybe it looked like that. There's a hole up above, right? Some sun shone down the hole and over the rocks."

"That wasn't just a bit of sun. Sun isn't blue."

"Look, Ammy —"

"It's Amelia!" There, she was back to normal.

She pushed past them and crawled out of the cave. Ike and Simon followed. The snow-reflected light out on the ledge was blinding. Ammy turned around at once and started lowering herself down over the lip of the ledge.

"She's right, y'know," Ike said. "Sun isn't blue. Besides, we all saw the blue light last night. And there wasn't any sun then."

"So what caused it?"

"UFO, obviously."

"Ike, seriously."

Ike sighed and thumped his hiking pole on the ledge. "There's nothing in there that could make a light like that. I'm out of ideas. What do *you* think?"

"I think we need to investigate. We need special equipment. A Geiger counter, maybe. It'll take some work."

§

The climb back up to the park at the end of Deacon Street was slower than the trip down, and much less exciting, which was the way Simon liked it. Once up top again, the first thing they did was walk back along the clifftop path to the spot above the cave.

"To confirm my theory about the footprints," Simon said, "we'll find the place where the guy took off the crampons."

Ike was already uncasing his camera.

They found the place on the cliff edge where the footprints appeared in the snow. But there were none of the dragging marks you'd get where a person had hauled himself over the edge. And no welter of marks where a person might have kneeled down or hopped on one foot to remove the crampons. No boot tracks leading away, either.

It looked just as if the person, whoever he was, had climbed the cliff and stepped onto the snow at the top without the help of a rope or even hands. And then walked away on his little steel points.

"This I've got to show my dad," Ike said, patting his camera case.

The trail led to a cedar hedge at the back of somebody's yard and disappeared through a gap at the bottom. It had left a trough scooped in the snow. "The marks go on past that house," Simon said, pulling his head and shoulders back.

Without having to discuss it — even Ammy seemed fascinated — they trotted along the path to Deacon Street, then around the block. Then stood, groaning, at the sight of neatly cleared sidewalks and salted road. They walked up and down the street on both sides, but the trail was lost.

Heads down, hands stuffed in pockets, they scuffed along Park Street towards the bridge across the gorge.

"Hey, Ammy!" Ike, always the first to perk up after a disappointment, dropped back level with her. "You still got that artifact?"

"The ring, he means," Simon said.

"I know what he means." Her gloved right hand clenched.

"Can I see it a minute?" Ike took off his mitt and held out his hand. Ammy looked like she was going to refuse, then shrugged, pulled off her glove, and handed him the ring. She'd been holding it against her palm. In the sun the stone blazed like fire. The scratches on it stood out clearly.

"There's a picture on it, a sort of cat's eye." Simon nudged it with his mitt as it lay on Ike's palm. "Maybe it's valuable after all. It could be a signet ring, like kings used to wear. To stamp papers with," he explained to Ike, who was looking puzzled. "To make things official."

"Your minute's up." Ammy reached for it.

Ike whisked it aside. "One more sec!" He knelt down and carefully wedged the band into the crack between two cement slabs, so that the stone shone up at them. Then he stood up, hefted his hiking pole, and stabbed it straight down at the stone. The steel point bounced back. Ammy shrieked and punched Ike in the shoulder so that he sprawled in the snow of somebody's lawn. She scooped up the ring and peered at it. "Don't you *ever* —" she began.

Simon leaned in for a better look. "Now, that's weird."

Ike was on his feet again. "Is it —"

"Not even cracked."

"You see? Looks like glass, but harder than steel. Obviously it's made of some exotic mineral not known on this planet."

"Ike, a ruby is harder than steel, and it's known on this planet."

"Well, maybe it's harder than that. We'll go and test it properly."

"How?"

"You are not touching it again!" Ammy shoved it into her jeans pocket.

"Diamond," Ike said across her to Simon.

"Where would you get a diamond?"

"I have my sources."

"You keep your paws off it." Ammy sidestepped them and clomped away up the street.

Ike and Simon followed her across the Queen Street bridge. The town hall clock bonged three times as they rounded the bend onto King Street. Ammy quickened her step. The next three blocks were already closed to traffic. People were stringing lights in the trees and hanging banners above the street: "DUNSTONE'S 15th ANNUAL NIGHT OF MAGIC." Other people were setting up booths along the sidewalk.

Ammy ignored the activity. She ignored Ike's pleading, too. He would have followed her into the lobby of the Hammer Block if Simon hadn't diverted him.

"C'mon, I could use a doughnut. And then let's ask your dad about those tracks, eh?"

"That's right!" Ike forgot about Ammy. "We've got proof, now. Pictures never lie. Dad can tell the police."

§

"Good pictures, Ike. Well composed, beautifully clear. Simon, keep that jelly doughnut away from my key-board, would you?" Oscar Vogelsang zoomed in on the image on his computer screen. Ike's father was huge, red-bearded, and untidy. Ike leaned on his left shoulder, beaming, while Simon edged in on the other side, hold-ing his doughnut out sideways.

"When are you going to call the police?" Ike asked.

"I'm not. Sorry." Oscar swivelled his chair to face him.

"But why not?"

"These pictures aren't proof of anything, let alone a UFO. You could have made those marks yourself."

"Dad, no!"

"We would never —" Simon started.

"I know, I know!" Oscar waved both hands. "Of course I believe you! But my belief isn't proof, you see? Certainly not to the police."

"Bummer." Ike picked up his camera. "So what do you think made those marks?"

Oscar swivelled back to look at the screen. He scratched his jaw through his beard. "Mm … a giant lizard?"

"Aw, Dad."

"Never mind, Ike. If you get a really good picture from the street party tonight I'll run it in the paper, how's that? I'll even pay you."

"Cool!"

Ike and Simon walked back past the service desk to the front of the office and stood at the window finishing their doughnuts. A young woman with short dark hair sat behind the desk tapping at a computer. "There's my diamond source," Ike said. "Melissa. New engagement ring."

The phone rang. Melissa snatched it up on the third ring. "*Dunstone Independent*. Yes, you are too late. You should have had it in before closing Saturday." She dropped the phone into its cradle and shook her head at Simon. "People! They know the deadline for placing ads, but they always push it."

"An ad. Right! Simon, that's what we should do."

"What are you talking about?"

"That artifact Ammy found. We should run an ad for her in the lost and found column."

Oscar sauntered over. "An ad? What did you lose?"

"It's just something my cousin Ammy found out on Riverside Drive yesterday," Simon said.

"Valuable?"

"Could be," Simon began.

Ike broke in. "It's a ring. We think the stone may be a gem. A ruby, maybe. It's harder than steel." He said to Simon out of the corner of his mouth, "I'd like a sight of the character that dropped it."

"It's too late to place an ad." Simon pointed at Melissa. "She just said so."

"Oh, I think we can squeeze in two lines for a neighbour," Oscar said.

Melissa looked at the clock. "No way, we're just about to send the disk to the printer."

"We can, if we're real quick. I'll take care of this, Melissa." He waved her away and sat down at her computer and started typing. "Found: December 30, Riverside Drive, small object, possibly valuable."

"Shouldn't we say what it is?" asked Simon. Then he smacked his forehead. "Of course not! Then we'd never know if the person is telling the truth."

"You got it." Oscar's fingers flew. "If confirmed, owner pays ad cost." He looked at Simon. "How about a phone number? Celeste's? Perfect. There, done — just in time, eh, Melissa? Two dollars, please. Best deal in the county."

CHAPTER TEN
MARA

The apartment was deserted when Simon returned. So was 3A. Simon found Ammy and her new friend on the roof. The girl sat cross-legged on the parapet at the front of the building, looking down at the street. The low-slanting sun and the wind caught her hair and it streamed out like a flame.

"Not again!" Simon said.

Ammy looked back over her shoulder and then crunched across the snow to meet him. "I think she just likes being in high places," she whispered. "Be cool. Don't scare her."

"*She* scares *me*."

The girl smiled back at them. "So much moving down there!" She waved a hand over the street. "What they do?"

"It's a party," Simon said. "To celebrate the first

night in the new year."

"Parrr-ty? Parrr-ty." She turned the word over in her mouth. Then spun herself around on the parapet, still cross-legged, and fixed her eyes on him. "Means what?"

"It's when people get together and have fun."

"Ah! Fun. What way they have fun?"

"Well, they play games, and dance, and skate. Stuff like that. There's music and food, too. And there are prizes for the best costumes."

"Coss-tumes."

"That's when you dress up," Ammy put in. "You disguise yourself. You make yourself look different."

The girl spun herself around again and bent at the waist to look down at the street. Simon's hand shot out. Ammy took a quick step forward.

"Blue, white, shining." The girl shaded her eyes. "So sharp!"

"What is?" Ammy bent over the parapet beside her. Simon grabbed the back of Ammy's jacket. She swatted his hand away.

"The colours of this — this place." The girl held out both arms. "So cold, so bright! Where I come from, the colours are soft and hot."

Aha, a clue! Simon poked Ammy in the arm. "So it's hot where you come from?"

"Yes, much. How I wish I know what happens there!"

He cleared his throat. "Um ... where is *there?*"

"My home." Her voice went flat.

"I give up!" Simon shoved his hands in his pockets and walked away. He stopped at the nearest chimney and kicked at the snow at its base. Then he stopped his foot in mid-kick, put it down, and studied the snow. "Uh-oh."

"How about coming inside?" Ammy coaxed. "You don't have a coat. Aren't you cold?"

"Ammy!" Simon broke in. "Over here!"

"It's *Amelia!*"

"Amelia. You'll want to see this."

"Oh, all right. What's the big deal?"

He pointed. Next to the chimney, where the snow was sheltered from the wind, a trail of scuffed footprints marked the surface. Some of them looked like they were wearing crampons. Beyond the chimney they faded into the blown powder.

"But that's just like…"

"Right. How did he get up on the roof?"

"Well, if he could climb out of the gorge…"

"But why is he still wearing the crampons? That's just weird." *Unless those aren't crampons*, he thought. *Unless those prints are his actual…* "Nah." He shook his head.

A long shadow fell across the snow. The girl stood beside them looking down. Her mouth widened slowly into a smile that bared all her teeth.

"I saw these marks somewhere else today." Simon watched her face. "You know them?"

"Yesss."

"Friend of yours?"

"Friend!" She threw back her head and laughed. "Amelia! We will go to this party. We will have fun!"

Still laughing, she strode towards the hut, with Amelia trotting at her heels. Simon dodged around in front of them. "I asked you a question!"

She grinned down at him. "Answer is no." She started around him. He sidestepped to stay in front of her.

Ammy grabbed his arm. "Simon, don't be a jerk!"

"Use your head! Last night there was a blue light in that cave, made by — who knows? Then she turns up, and I know for sure she's new — this town is small enough that I'd know. Then today we find those prints by the cave. And now we find them here."

"And that means what?"

"Add it up! She's part of some kind of..." He waved his hands in frustration. He had no idea what she was up to. But it smelled of secrets, of trickery. "Some kind of plot!"

"What is plot?" asked the girl.

He swung back to face her. Blinking at him like she didn't know anything! He was mad enough to stare her down — if only he were six inches taller. "A plot is people sneaking around to make trouble for other people. You in politics, back home?"

"Politics." Her smile twisted. "I know that word from radio. You would call it politics."

"Wow." Ammy sounded admiring. "Aren't you awfully young to be in politics?"

"Six days ago, I was too young."

"What hap—" Ammy began, but Simon couldn't let her finish.

"Those marks?" He pointed at the snow. "What made them?"

The girl's eyes sparkled. "He comes from my brother."

"So, he is a friend!"

"No. This means my brother is not having things so easy, back home!" Her lips quirked.

"Then he's a messenger?" Ammy ventured. "He brings news?"

"He wants you to come home?" Simon suggested.

"That, no!" She laughed.

Enough is enough! He met the girl stare for stare. "Look — we kept our promise. We haven't told any-body. So why can't you be honest with us?"

"Hon-est?"

"Honest! I mean, we don't even know your name, and you know ours. Is that fair?"

The girl stared down at him from what suddenly

seemed a great height. Her head slanted back, her face looked longer and sharper. Her eyes were two green slits. *Now I've done it,* he thought. *Now she's really mad!* There was a crunch as Ammy stepped up beside him.

For a moment nobody breathed. Then the girl sighed and he'd have sworn she'd shrunk down again by eight or ten inches. "Where I come from it is not a small thing, the telling of names. But you are right. I … what is the word … I owe. I owe you, Amelia." She touched Ammy's arm. "I was a … a stranger. And you were friend. You could let me die in the snow, last night."

"No, I couldn't!"

"We couldn't!" Simon added.

"I would not die, of course. I do not die so easy. But you did not know that. So…" She held out her hands. "My name is" — she took a breath — "Marathynarradin."

"Mara…thar…" Simon tried. "Marathin…"

"Marin…" Ammy said. "Say again?"

"Marathynarradin," the girl said firmly, as if she'd made up her mind about something.

"We'll call you Mara for short," Ammy said.

"For short!" Mara's eyes narrowed. "You would cut my name?"

"Sure, why not? Mara's a cute name."

"Cute." Mara frowned down at her angora- and jean-clad length and let out a bark of laughter. "Why not? I am less, so why should my name not be less? Let it be Mara, then."

"Good." Ammy took her hand and tugged. "Can we go down now?"

"Yes, now!" Mara led the parade towards the hut. "There is a party. We disguise ourself."

Simon crunched through the snow behind them. "You know, it's funny how fast your English has got better."

"Amelia gives me a radio. I talk, it doesn't answer, so I listen. I learn. But most I learn from Amelia."

"But where'll we find costumes?" Ammy followed her into the hut and down the stairs. "Wait, I know! Those boxes in 3A. There's got to be something there we can use."

"You can't! That stuff is for Boomer Heaven!"

"Simon, it'll be okay. Go and ask Grandmother if we can dress up, just for tonight. Say we'll be really careful."

"Right," he said. "Careful." He felt he was the only person around here who knew the meaning of the word. As he thumped down the stairs behind them, he realized: they knew Mara's name now, but that was all they knew. Nothing about where she came from or what she was up to. Once again, she'd avoided giving a straight answer.

He didn't trust her an inch.

CHAPTER ELEVEN
NIGHT OF MAGIC

They'd been out on the street about an hour before Amelia realized someone was following them.

She might have noticed earlier, only there was so much to see and do. Dunstone's Night of Magic had turned out to be more fun than she'd expected. After the sun went down, the three closed-off blocks of King Street filled up with what looked like the town's entire population.

A band played on a stage in front of the town hall steps. Lights strung in the bare trees and between the buildings roofed the street with a golden haze. There were booths selling fries and hot dogs and apple fritters. And everywhere you looked there were buskers — a woman who played a violin, a man who juggled knives and flaming torches, three clowns who joined up to make a giant wheel and rolled around the pavement.

Mara stared wide-eyed. "I really wonder about where she comes from," Simon said in Amelia's ear. She wondered too. Everything seemed new to Mara. It wasn't just like she'd never seen clowns before, or people chipping blocks of ice into the shapes of mermaids and horses and the CN Tower, or an illusionist pulling a rabbit out of a hat. It was like she'd never even heard of clowns or ice or people who did magic tricks — never knew there were such things. She was surprised when the magician didn't *eat* the rabbit.

She'd get upset at the strangest things. When the juggler started to blow plumes of fire from his mouth, Mara growled in her throat and began stalking through the crowd towards him. Amelia caught up with her and held her arm while Simon explained that the man wasn't really breathing fire — it was just a gas that he set alight, and he'd smeared his face and mouth with some gunk to keep from being burned.

"So it is not real." Mara's arm relaxed.

"That's right. It's pretend."

Mara attracted a lot of attention herself. Wherever you looked, somebody was staring or pointing. It wasn't that her outfit was so astonishing. There were plenty of goofy costumes, and a few clever ones, and lots of masks, including the usual vampires and ghouls and politicians.

One mask was actually scary, Amelia thought, though she couldn't figure out what it was supposed to be. The face was sickly white, almost silver, and the area around the eyeholes deeply shadowed. Eyes glittered in the shadows. The second time she glimpsed it, the person slipped away before she could point it out to Mara and Simon.

Mara was magnificent. She wore a long, sequin-covered coat that looked like a lizard's skin, if that lizard happened to be bright red. Her hair streamed from under a scarf of gauzy gold wrapped around her head like a crown. Over her shoulders hung a silk shawl, all flame-like patterns of scarlet and orange and crimson, that spread like wings when she raised her arms. She looked as if she might take flight any moment — and burst into fire in mid-air.

They found Ike Vogelsang snapping pictures of a small kid having her face painted. Simon tapped him on the shoulder, and he turned around. His mouth dropped open.

"Wow! Who's that?"

"Um … Mara. Friend of Ammy's."

"Really? Hi! What's the costume?"

"Amelia says I am firebird."

"No kidding. Then what are you, Ammy — a Honda Civic?" Ike punched Simon in the arm and the two of them snorted with laughter.

"A firebird," Amelia said haughtily, "is a bird that burns itself to death, and then comes back to life again.

It gets born again out of its own ashes. And I…" She twirled to show off the shiny black plastic jacket that she'd stuffed herself into after pulling on two sweaters, and the headband trimmed with black feathers that she'd fastened around a black toque. "I'm the Raven Nevermore. So watch out!"

"Nevermore. Right, we took that. Poe." Ike focused on Mara and clicked. Then he frowned at the image display. "Darn it."

"Why aren't you dressing up?" Amelia asked.

"I'm on assignment. How 'bout you, Simon?"

"Me? I'm just here to keep an eye on Ammy."

"*Amelia*. And I don't need a babysitter!"

"Celeste said we're to stay together and I'm to watch out for you. So that's what I'm doing. Like it or not."

In spite of Simon, it was fun. Amelia had to admit that. She bought light sticks for all of them and used hers to write her initials in big, glowing letters in the air. She bought cardboard glasses with prismatic lenses that turned all the lights into rainbows. (Mara tore hers off after one look.) Simon paid for cups of steaming sweet cider, and Ike, with silly bows and flourishes, handed around little paper bags of roasted chestnuts. Mara would have eaten hers whole if Simon hadn't showed her how to pry the white nuts out of the smoking husks.

There were clothing vendors to browse, too. Boomer Heaven had a booth across from the town hall, with fringed suede vests, macramé belts, and strings of love beads (according to the sign) for sale. And there behind the table was Celeste, with reindeer antlers on her head and a glowing Rudolph nose, making change for a customer.

Amelia took Mara by one arm and Simon took the other and they hurried her across the street before Celeste could spot them and start wondering about the tall girl in the vintage red-sequined coat.

Once they were out of sight Simon dropped Mara's arm and walked away a few steps, glowering at the pavement. "This feels rotten," he said.

"What does?" Ike joined them, camera in hand. "I just got a good shot of your grandmother in her antlers. Wish I could get one of Ammy's friend, there, but look." He held out the camera. "She keeps moving or something. All I ever get is a blur."

Simon gave Mara a suspicious look. She smiled at him.

"It's not like she does it on purpose," Amelia said.

"No?" He stepped into a doorway, out of the stream of people, to peer at Ike's camera.

"Look at that guy!" Ike pointed with his chin. "Over there — this side of the stage. That's some mask! I better get a shot of him." He squirmed through the crowd to find Simon.

Amelia looked where he'd been pointing. It was the scary mask again. It was the eyes that did it, she figured.

In the shadowy sockets they sparkled as bright as the edge of a knife blade. A phrase sidled into her head: *Kill you soon as look at you.*

Below the mask was a long, thin body dressed in greyish stuff that looked like he'd scrounged it out of a dumpster. He was watching her, she was sure of it. Or watching... "Mara? I think ... There, he's gone again."

"I know." Mara glanced in that direction. "He follows us since we come outside."

"You knew? Who is he? Oh, wait. It's that guy your brother sent, right? The messenger."

"Not messenger. I have been searching for the word for him. I hear it today on the radio. It begins *Ah*."

"Assistant?"

"No."

"Advisor?"

"No. Now I have it! Ah...sah...sin." She popped the last peeled chestnut into her mouth and crunched.

"A..." Ammy gaped at Mara. "Assassin? Your brother sent a hit man?"

"*The* Assassin." The way Mara said it, you could hear the capital *A*. "A good sign. A sign of how much my brother fears me."

A knot of boys jostled past. Amelia grabbed Mara's arm and hustled her out of the crowd, where anybody could come up next to you before you noticed, to the pool of quiet next to the chestnut roaster's charcoal grill.

"He knows where we live!" Amelia hissed. "He was on our roof!"

Mara settled her shawl around her shoulders. "That was just to warn me. Or else we would not see his marks. He would not be so clumsy."

"But why would he warn you?"

"He has some pride, this one. He is the Assassin. Not just a killer."

The chestnut man looked at them sideways. Amelia led Mara a little farther away, then planted herself in front of her. "This is where we show some sense and go to the police."

"No! You promised not to tell."

"But this guy wants to kill you!" Amelia looked around wildly. "And what about all these people? What about Grandmother, and Simon, and … and…"

Mara waved a careless hand. "He only wants to kill me."

"That's bad enough! How can you be so calm?"

"Because he is in danger too." Her teeth gleamed. "From me."

Amelia shivered. For the first time tonight, she felt how useless the plastic jacket was against this bone-cracking cold, even with two sweaters underneath. "At least let's get inside, away from this crowd."

CHAPTER TWELVE
ASSASSIN

Amelia felt at home the minute they stepped into the new mall, the one Simon had pointed out so proudly the day before. It was small — didn't even have a movie theatre — but in many ways it was like every other mall she'd ever been in, with walls that looked like marble but probably weren't, and plenty of stainless steel and shining glass, and small trees in pots under skylights. It smelled of new clothes, fresh paint, and cinnamon buns. Amelia inhaled deeply.

Hardly any people were here. Almost everybody else was out in the street, enjoying the party. That was good. If that Assassin — *This can't be happening!* — if he followed them in here, they'd spot him a mile away. Or at least the length of the corridor away.

"What is that?" Mara was staring, head high, eyes narrowed, at a man in a burgundy blazer and grey pants, as tall as Amelia's father but twice as wide, standing next to the automatic teller. He stared back with stony eyes.

"Mall cop," Amelia whispered. "Don't look at him. We're window shopping, got that?"

The cop turned his head slowly as Amelia and Mara strolled by. Amelia walked stiffly until they were around the corner and out of sight. "Those guys hate kids," she muttered. "Give him any excuse and he'll throw us out."

"Ah!" Mara tossed back her hair. "Good! Then we fight!" She spun on the spot and headed back the way they'd come.

Amelia dashed after her. "No! Are you crazy?"

Mara sighed. "Yes … yes, you are wise." She turned back and fell into step beside Amelia again. "I am too old now for such play. But, oh…" She stretched, spreading her shawl into wings. "How I wish for a good fight!"

Amelia shook her head. Either Simon was right and Mara was crazy, or she'd had a very strange upbringing. "Let's just be cool. Look at these, aren't they pretty?" A rack of rhinestone earrings, 50 percent off, stood outside a store called Eleganz. Amelia didn't think much of them — too dangly and fussy — but anything to distract Mara. The clerk watched them from inside the store. Amelia gave her a polite smile and walked on.

A moment later something cool slid into her hand. She stopped and looked. A card with a pair of rhinestone earrings in it glittered up at her.

"For you." Mara smiled. "A — what is the word? A present."

"Uh … Mara…"

"You don't like?"

"Did you pay for them? Of course you didn't. No time." She met Mara's puzzled eyes. "Besides, you don't even know about money, do you?"

"Money?"

"Hey! You two!"

The mall cop was coming after them at a run. Amelia hesitated only a split second. Mara was already starting to turn back, eyes bright. Amelia threw the earrings as hard as she could back along the corridor and snatched Mara's hand. "Run!"

Mara laughed as she ran. Amelia sprinted to keep up. Heavy feet thudded behind. "He's … gonna … catch us!" This was awful. Any second now they'd be arrested for shoplifting and Grandmother would tell her parents, and…

"Then we slow him down."

Mara darted at a storefront. Pets Galore, said the overhead sign. She plunged her hand into a glass tank standing beside the entrance. Amelia jogged on the spot. "Mara, put that back!"

"Go," Mara said to the tiny thing in her hand. "Go and be many." She set it down gently on the floor. It was a spotted lizard.

"You girls! Stop!"

Amelia grabbed Mara's hand again and dragged her away.

The corridor behind them filled with flickery sounds, like thousands of tiny feet on tile. Amelia grabbed a look over her shoulder. The floor and walls were ... moving. *I didn't see that!* She faced front and sprinted on. Two seconds later somebody behind them screamed.

They skidded around a corner and burst across an open space filled with little round tables and chairs. The food court. A few people were here, mostly near the Espresso Bar. Cups stopped halfway to lips as Amelia and Mara dashed past.

Amelia looked back again. "There's another one after us — and — his eyes —"

"Yes, I saw." Mara wasn't even out of breath. "The eyes are the last thing to change."

"He's — your — Assass—" She slid to a halt, because Mara had stopped short. Amelia's feathered headband dipped over her eyes. She pushed it back.

"Look, Amelia — firebird!" Mara's voice rang out across the food court. She pointed a long finger at the Espresso Bar. A big shiny chrome espresso machine stood on the counter. On top was the brass eagle that Simon had boasted about. People on both sides of the counter gaped at them.

The mall cop with the strange, too-bright eyes was walking towards them now. He must think they were already in the bag. And in a couple of seconds they would be.

"Mara, let's go!"

"Firebird will fight for us." Mara crooked her finger. The espresso machine rocked from side to side. Heads turned. Amelia stood staring until Mara seized her hand and dragged her towards the glass doors that led to the street.

This time she had no chance to look back. Behind them, somebody shrieked, and somebody else yelled *Oh my god*, and a cup smashed on tile. And then a horrible yowl, like the cry of a gigantic cat, drowned them out.

Mara burst into laughter as she bounded out into the crowded street.

"What happened?" Amelia gasped. "Who got hurt?"

"Him! Ha, first blood goes to me! Now he will chase with a whole heart!"

"And that's good?"

"Yes! Now we run for true!"

§

"How many?" Simon echoed.

"Thousands of them," said the pet store owner. He waved a hand at the corridor outside his store. "Just like that one in the tank. That's the only one I could catch."

"Leopard geckos," Ike scribbled in his pocket notebook.

Simon looked around. "So, where are they all?"

"No idea. But they were here." The man flapped wildly at the floor and walls and ceiling. "They were!"

Ike slipped his notebook back into his pocket. "Dad'll have to print this. Thousands of lizards! Out of nowhere!"

It got worse. In the food court, the talk was all about two girls who ran through five minutes ago, one of them tall and dressed in glittering red. And what she called out, and what happened next.

Ike took a picture of the espresso machine with the brass eagle on top. He tried to get the store manager, Danny Chaves, to stand beside the machine, but Danny refused. Nobody wanted to be anywhere near it, he said.

"Looks safe enough to me." Simon went up close to the machine and examined the eagle. It looked exactly the same as he remembered. There was no sign it had ever broken away from its perch.

"It flew," Danny insisted. "It attacked a security guard."

"Him?" Simon pointed at a big man in a burgundy jacket who was talking on a cell phone.

"No, the other one. The one who ran out after the girls."

"That's funny. I didn't think...." He walked over to the guard and waited until he lowered the cell phone. "Excuse me. Where's the other guard?"

"What other guard?"

"That's what I thought." Simon headed for the doors.

"What d'you think?" Ike was at his elbow. "Did everybody go crazy at once? Did Mara hypnotize them? What?"

"Maybe."

"Something's going on and you know about it, don't you? What's the big secret?"

Simon stopped just short of the doors and faced him. "I ... I can't say." Not until Mara let him out of that promise. He wished he'd kept his mouth shut, that time.

Ike had that freckles-standing-out-all-over look. "I'm not playing now. And I know you're not. That girl, Mara — it's about her, isn't it?" He held up his camera case. "You saw."

Simon nodded. Ike had taken three pictures of him, Ammy, and Mara standing side by side with cups of cider in their hands. He and Ammy and everything else were in perfect focus, but Mara beside them was just a blur.

"And now this." Ike waved at the mall. "Why can't you tell me?"

"Because right now there's no time!"

"Okay. If that's the way you want it." Ike turned his back and stalked away.

Simon started to call after him, then decided to save his breath. Straightening things out with Ike would have to wait. He pushed through the glass door into the street.

Stick together and keep an eye on Ammy, Celeste had said. And now Ammy was out with Mara, which was a worry all by itself, and some guy was chasing them who looked like a mall cop but wasn't.

He had to find them before something awful happened. But... He looked back and forth and through the laughing crowd. Which way?

CHAPTER THIRTEEN
TO THE EDGE OF THE WORLD

Amelia had never run before as she ran now, hand in hand with Mara. The street whizzed under her feet. People's faces were blurred ovals with black gaps in them. The shouts came a second later.

In two thudding heartbeats they were past the street party barriers and bounding straight up the centre of King Street. Car horns blared around them, pickups veered aside. Like magic, Amelia thought. Like everything had to obey the wave of Mara's hand.

They hardly touched down, just skimmed the surface — so Amelia's boot soles told her. (The new boots that had weighed like lead when she bought them and now weighed like feathers. *Anti-gravity boots*, she thought dizzily.) When potholes gaped beneath her feet she leaped, and then, for moments that stretched out long and dreamlike, she was flying, she'd swear it.

Without warning Mara swerved right and cut along an alley between houses. Amelia veered with her like a bird in a flock of two. The built-up spaces between the streets didn't even slow them down. They sprang from a low roof onto snow, burst into and out of a thicket of trees...

And there it ended. Ahead of them lay a plain of silver stretching towards the sky. Beyond the field was nothing but stars. *We can't go any farther*, Amelia thought. *We've run to the edge of the world.*

She stumbled and stopped. While she was bent over, hands on knees, panting, the magic drained away. A bent black feather fell from her headband and stuck point-down in the snow.

She straightened up. They stood on an ice-rutted sidewalk lined with trees. Streetlights glimmered through bare branches. Behind them stood a row of small houses, mostly dark. Seemed like everybody really was downtown.

The silver plain across the street was just a park, white snow rising to a long, low hilltop. They'd run to the edge of Dunstone, not the world.

"Mara, what" — Amelia gulped for air — "what hap-happened back there? In the mall? Was that something you did?"

Mara didn't answer. Amelia looked where she was looking, along the street to their right. Someone was walking towards them. The figure appeared in a pool of streetlight, crossed it, and faded into the dark.

"Go home." Mara took her by the shoulders and pushed her away.

"It's him, isn't it? The Assassin. Right, let's go!"

"You go. I stay."

Amelia spun around. The walker was passing through another pool of light, closer. The light reflected off eyes like broken ice. Two more steps, and he was invisible in the dark.

"Mara, you can't stay! Come on!" She grabbed Mara's arm and pulled. It was like pulling a tree: there was some give, but it got you nowhere.

For half a moment Amelia thought, *I should get away. She's crazy. She's dangerous.* Then: *No! She's in danger. I can't leave her.*

"Mara! There's still time if we run!"

"Did you think I ran for fear? I ran to bring him here, away from people."

"But he'll kill you!"

"We will see." Mara folded her arms and smiled, showing teeth. She had lost her shawl somewhere and her red lizard coat glittered in the streetlight. "Maybe I can make him talk to me instead. He knows things I must know."

"But you can't do this by yourself! I can help. I — I can fight!" Amelia looked around for a branch, a broken piece of fence, anything. Ten seconds and he'd be here —

Amelia. The name echoed back and forth through her mind. *Brave Amelia. This fight is not for you.*

Her mind was full of glare. She shut her eyes.

When she opened them again the street was deserted, except for herself. Her right hand was in her pocket, closed tight around the ruby ring. Its warmth beat like a heart against her fingers.

§

Simon found Ammy on Hill Street on the north edge of town, staring across the street at Founders Park. She whirled and backed away as he trudged near, then let out a huge sigh of relief.

"How did you find me?"

"Celeste's shawl, to start." He held up the wad of silk. "The chestnut man picked it up and hung it on his cart. He told me which way you guys went. After that I just kept asking people if they'd seen two crazy girls run by." He looked past her, then around. "Where's Mara?"

"I don't know. I'm afraid she's going to get killed."

"That guy who was chasing you —"

"That was the Assassin."

"The what?"

She explained. Long before she finished he was shaking his head.

"This is Dunstone. We don't get hit men here."

"We got Mara."

"That's true." He thought of the geckos and the espresso eagle. "And nothing's been really normal ever since."

"She's in trouble. I can't wait here." She started across the street.

"Wait a minute! Where you going?"

"To find her." She headed into the park. Simon hurried after her. Their boots broke through the snow crust at each step.

"But we don't even know which way she's gone! Where are her tracks?"

Ammy tramped on, hands in the pockets of her plastic jacket. "You don't have to come."

"D'you know what Celeste will do to me if I come home without you?"

They climbed the hill, floundered down the other side into deep snow at the bottom, then struggled up the farther slope. They were still climbing when a reddish light flushed the sky.

"Fireworks?" Simon wondered aloud. It looked like sheet lightning, only it was the wrong colour. And the wrong season. "Fire?"

When they reached the top of the hill there was

nothing to see but miles of tree-fuzzed darkness streaked with ghostly white. No fire. And no smell, sight, or sound of fireworks.

"What makes you so sure she's out there?" Simon asked.

"She came here to get him away from people, she said. That's where she'd go — out there, where there's nothing but snow and trees. Nobody to be hurt."

Red light flared in the distance behind a fold of the hills.

"What *is* that?" Simon muttered. "Flares? Flame-throwers?"

"Whatever it is, I'm afraid for Mara."

"I bet she can take care of herself."

They stood and watched the dark land below them. After a few minutes Ammy said, "She called me 'Brave Amelia.' Me!"

"Why not you?"

"Because I was shaking like jelly, that's how brave I was!"

"So you were scared. Who wouldn't be? I mean, a hit man!"

"Mara wasn't scared. I wish I was more like her."

"I'm glad you're not! She said she was mixed up in politics, remember? If this is politics where she comes from — assassins and flame-throwers and hypnotizing people — I hope she doesn't come back."

Ammy turned her back on him. "Fine. You go home. I'll wait."

"I can't go home without you."

They stood a couple of metres apart, stamping their feet to keep warm, with Ammy pretending he wasn't there. After about five minutes she walked over and stood beside him and said in a small voice that got smaller as she spoke, "I'm afraid for her because he — the Assassin — I'm afraid he's … not … human."

Simon went colder still, but he tried to sound sure of himself. "You mean, the footprints."

"And other things. Like how he changed. In the street he was thin and grey and in the mall he looked just like a mall cop, big and wide, only … the eyes were the same. Like, like knife edges. And Mara said, 'The eyes are the last thing to change.'"

"So, where she comes from there are people who can change their shape. That must be pretty, um, rare."

They stood in silence, except for the squeak of feet in snow, for another few minutes. Then he said, "And Mara can do strange things to people's minds. I don't think that brass eagle actually flew. I think she made them think it flew."

"Mm. Yeah," Ammy said, and shifted from foot to foot, and watched the hills.

"Being able to do things like that must be pretty rare, too."

"Yeah." After another long pause Ammy said, "Mara didn't even know about money. Everybody knows about money. And she…"

"She what?"

"Oh, nothing, just … I didn't even see her leave. She was just gone."

"I wouldn't have thought anybody could really do stuff like that. I mean" — Simon blew his breath out in a long plume — "not anybody on Earth."

They waited and watched until they couldn't feel their feet. No more fire, or fireworks, lit up the hills. Mara didn't come back.

CHAPTER FOURTEEN
A FACE AT THE WINDOW

After they got home, Amelia opened her laptop. Still no message from her parents. She fired off an email.

Dear Mom and Dad, where are you? Are you all right? Did you get my first email? Please write AS SOON AS YOU GET THIS!!! Love, Amelia.

There was a message from Silken, though. Amelia hadn't even thought of Silken all day, and she felt guilty.

Hi Silken. I have had an incredible day. This girl

She stopped. No, can't write about Mara. That would be the same as telling. She deleted *This girl* and began again. *I went rock climbing with Simon and his friend Ike. It's more interesting than you'd think. I explored a cave and*

And what? What was that light in the cave?

later we went out to this First Night party in the street. It was kind of fun.

All that didn't add up to an incredible day. Amelia deleted *an incredible* and put in *a nice*. Lame, but the best she could do. Then added, *How about you?* and signed off.

She fell asleep thinking of Mara. Where was she? Was she all right?

In dreams she soared again above the jagged red landscape. The winged creatures leaped up at her from pinnacles and tower tops. She beat upward, easily out-distanced them, circled back, and dove. They scattered away from her like leaves in the wind. *Ha, cowards!* Fire burst across her vision. The whole sky turned red.

She woke and lay gasping. Her right hand cramped. She uncurled the fingers and the ruby ring slid out onto the blanket. She pushed it under the pillow.

At least I'm in my own bed this time! she thought.

The room wasn't all that dark. She had left the curtains open and the glow from the streetlights poured in. Turning away from the window didn't help much. A bright square lit up the wall a few inches away from her face.

Amelia closed her eyes. That didn't help much either, but she didn't want to close the curtains. The memory of being shut in the pitch-dark stairwell last night still made her shiver.

The glow through her eyelids darkened. She opened her eyes. The yellow square on the wall had a black shape cut out of it.

I'm dreaming. She turned over in bed and looked at the window. There it was again. A black shadow hanging from the top of the window. Long shadow arms reached to the sides of the window frame. At the bottom, two eyes glittered at her out of the black silhouette.

I don't like this dream. Wake up! She smacked herself in the face. *Wake — up!*

Amelia sat straight up in bed. The shadow at the window bent an arm. Sharp fingers scratched at the frame.

She flung back her head and screamed, "Gran!" And hurled herself out of bed and across the room. The door flew open, nearly hitting her in the nose, and Grandmother was there.

"Sh-sh-sh! It's all right!"

"There was —" Amelia realized she was clinging to Grandmother's warm, rayon-covered, sandalwood-smelling arms like a two-year-old. She detached herself and pointed at the window. "There was something at the window looking in at me!" No shadow hung there now.

Simon was in the room now too. He went over to the window and looked out and down. "Couldn't be. You have no fire escape."

"It was hanging from the top of the window — upside down." Somehow that made it more horrible.

Like a great big bat. "I think" — she took a deep breath — "I think it was the Assassin."

Grandmother made a "Tch!" sound. Simon jerked the curtains closed.

"That was some dream," Grandmother said. "Want to come in with me for the duration?"

"Y..." Amelia began. Then thought: *How big a baby am I? Would Mara go crying to her gran? You can bet not.* She stood up straight and found her most grown-up tone of voice. "No, thank you, Grandmother. I'll be fine."

"You're sure?"

"Absolutely."

After lying awake for an hour, listening for noises at the window, Amelia went and got her laptop and crawled back into bed with it. This time, when she opened her email, it went "ding!" The subject line was "Here we are safe and sound." She blew out a huge *whuff!* of relief.

It was a long letter, all about airports and terrible roads and interesting people and centipedes of amazing size in the bathroom (Amelia suspected her father had put that in just to scare her off) and summer heat (*Right, it's near the equator*) as well as cold nights (*I get it, up in the mountains*). And they would write every day if they could, and they loved her very much and they knew she would behave her very best and do her share of the chores and be a friend to Simon.

Not a word about when she could join them in Peru. Perhaps they hadn't had time to really read her messages yet.

She typed:

mom and dad i am so homesick i mean homesick for you not vancouver i miss you i don't want to be here

Then she thought, *Mara. She needs my help. Of course I can't go to Peru yet! Besides, Mara wouldn't be such a crybaby. So I won't be, either.*

She deleted what she'd typed. Then:

Dear Mom and Dad, I'm glad you got there safe. I am being very nice to Simon and after all he isn't so bad. Just kind of geeky. I miss you very much and still hope to join you if we can fix it up. But give me a few days, maybe a week. There is something important I need to do here first. Lots of love, Amelia.

After that she slept.

§

The window rattled. Amelia flung off the covers and rolled out of bed on the side next to the wall. A cold white light seeped around the edges of the curtains.

Something was out there. What would Mara do?

Check it out. That's what she'd do.

Amelia crawled around the end of the bed — although she was pretty sure Mara wouldn't crawl — and across the room to the window. The frame rattled again, and something made flicking noises on the pane. Her breath came short and her throat tightened.

Here goes…

She reached up and pulled one curtain open. A raging whiteness filled the window. Snow! No, blizzard. She stood up and looked out. Couldn't see the buildings on the other side of the street. The streetlights bounced in the wind.

One good thing, even the Assassin would stay under cover today. Wouldn't he?

Then Amelia thought: *Mara. Is she out in that?*

She glanced at the ceiling. Then pulled on jeans, socks, and a sweater and headed out. The apartment was silent and deserted. The clock in the kitchen said nine-thirty. She let herself out, careful to leave the deadbolt off, and ran up the stairs to 3A. The door was locked, and there was no answer when she knocked and called.

The roof, then. But would Mara be on the roof in a blizzard?

Sure she would.

Amelia was halfway up the dim back stairs when the

door at the top swung open, letting in a steel grey light, a wave of snow, and Simon.

"No, she's not there." He shook snow off his jacket. "And neither are her clothes."

"Clothes?" Amelia retreated down the stairs.

"I was lying awake last night, thinking," he said as he clumped along the corridor, shedding snow at every step. "Trying to come up with answers to a lot of questions. Like, how did Mara get up on our roof with no clothes on? So I went up to look for the clothes. No luck."

"Maybe she threw them over the side."

"I'm checking that now." He thumped down the front stairs.

"Wait!"

He didn't wait, but Amelia (coated, booted, hatted, gloved, and scarved) caught up with him three minutes later. He was wading through drifts of snow in the alley beside the Hammer Block, scraping at the hidden pavement with his feet. She watched as he shuffled from one side of the alley to the other, eyes squinted against waves of blowing snow.

"If we don't find Mara's clothes, that won't prove anything," she said. "Somebody could have taken them."

"But if we do find them, that proves something."

"I'll start on the other side."

They met at the back of the building next to the

dumpster, having found nothing but a few empty beer cans. Then Simon spent five minutes trying to reach the bottom rung of the fire escape by jumping. In his heavy boots and parka he missed by several feet. Amelia did no better.

"But Mara's taller, and I bet she can jump higher." She thought of the run last night. Now, it seemed like another dream of flying. "A lot higher."

"Maybe." Simon led the way back up to the apartment. "So here's the theory: Mara sneaks into the building in the afternoon — it has to be then because the front door's locked at night — and up the back stairs to the roof. No, wait a minute. The door to the roof was bolted on the inside."

"So she must've come up by the fire escape."

"Okay. Then she gets undressed and throws her clothes over the side. Somebody finds them and takes them away. She waits in the cold like that until we find her." He gave Amelia a look. "That's crazy, but at least it's possible."

"Why are you so worried about things being possible? I mean, weird things do happen." They were back in the apartment now, shedding their boots and coats.

"Yeah, but things don't happen for no reason," Simon said. "Even the weird things. They're just harder to figure out."

"Like, about the Assassin?"

"And like about Mara. Yes."

"Mara's strange, she's not weird." Amelia headed for the kitchen. Her stomach was grumbling for food. "I'm more bothered about what's happened to her. She could be dead!"

"I bet not." Simon opened the refrigerator. "Why else would the Assassin visit you last night?"

"Of course!" Amelia laughed. "He must've been looking for her. It means she's alive!" Then she frowned. "But she could be hurt, and freezing, out in this weather."

"We could call the police." He carried eggs and milk and cheese and bread to the kitchen counter. "Ask them to search."

"But then we'd have to tell them everything! And we can't!"

"Then think of Mara on the roof in her birthday suit. If anyone would be okay in a blizzard, she'd be the one. I'm making a cheese omelet, want some?"

Amelia felt better with a stomach full of cheese omelet. "You really aren't such a kid anymore, are you? Sounds like you've worked out all the answers."

He flushed but pretended to be cool. "No way. I've just started asking some of the right questions." He swallowed a forkful of omelet. "Like, where does the Assassin come from, really? And does Mara come from the same place?"

"You think … not Earth." She put down her fork, not hungry anymore. "You sound like Ike. This isn't possible."

"It's not *im*possible. You know what Carl Sagan said."

"Who's Carl Sagan?"

He stared at her, mouth open, then rolled his eyes up and sighed. For Simon, that was an explosion. "Carl Sagan," he explained in his most patient tone, "was a great scientist. He figured out that there could be intelligent life on a million planets in our galaxy alone."

"Okay." Amelia sipped her juice. "And what are the odds of them turning up here?"

"Um, I don't know. Probably much lower."

"Do you believe in magic?"

"'Course not!" He laughed. "You don't, do you?"

"I don't know." She thought of her run with Mara through the streets last night. That had been magic, while it lasted. But had the magic only happened in her head?

"The thing that really gets me is the blue light you saw in the cave." Simon looked at his watch, glanced at the phone, and reached for more toast. "I think you saw something there."

"Well, of course I saw something! I just don't know what. Or why. Or how."

"They're all tied together — the blue light, the cave, the Assassin, Mara. I think we should go back and really search that cave."

"I think so too." She rapped him on the wrist. "Why do you keep looking at your watch?"

"Oh, no reason."

The phone rang. Simon shoved back his chair and lunged across the room.

CHAPTER FIFTEEN
A VOICE ON THE PHONE

Ike was on the line. "Any calls?"

"Not yet. Is the *Independent* out?"

"Yeah, it came out ten minutes ago. People will be calling any time now. You stick by the phone."

"That's what I'm doing." Simon glanced across the room to where Ammy was eating toast and watching him. It had occurred to him that she still didn't know he and Ike had published an ad about her ring. Considering how touchy she was about the thing, it might not be a good idea for her to find out by answering the phone. "I'll stick by it, you bet. So, you're not mad anymore?"

"You going to let me in on the secret?"

"What secret?"

Ike hung up.

"I wonder if Mara knows how to use the telephone?" Ammy said. "I'd better stay close in case she calls."

"Don't worry. You can go watch TV or something." Simon cleared the dishes from the table. "I'll get you if she calls," he said casually over his shoulder, from the sink.

"I don't feel like TV." She joined him at the sink and picked up a dish towel — *without even being asked*, he thought approvingly.

"I guess I should admit I was wrong, too." He fished a mug out of the suds and scrubbed at a tea stain.

"'Bout what?"

"'Bout you. You're much nicer when you're thinking about somebody besides yourself."

"When have I ever been not nice?"

He was still trying to figure out if she was joking when the phone rang. He dropped the mug into the suds with a splash and leaped, but Ammy, two steps closer to the phone, got there first. "Ad?" she said. "What ad? Today's paper? But we didn't…. Oh." She listened. "I guess we did." She sliced a look at Simon. "No, this is the right number. What did you lose? A gold owl off a charm bracelet. No, that isn't what we found. Sorry."

She hung up and crossed her arms at him. "So. Whose bright idea was it?"

"Um, both of ours." Her mouth opened; he rushed on. "Look, it's not like it's really yours. Somebody else lost it, and it's probably valuable, and it's only right —"

"But that's for me to decide! I bet Ike's got some silly plan. I thought you were too old to be playing games like this."

"What games are these?" Celeste breezed into the kitchen with a sheaf of advertising flyers under her arm.

"Simon!" Ammy waved her dish towel. "Thinks he can do what he likes with my stuff."

The phone rang. Celeste picked it up, flyers still under her arm. "Hammer. Hello, Vern. What can I do for you? Your car? What would I be doing with your car?" She listened, while her eyes flicked from Ammy to Simon. Then she muffled the receiver against her sweater. "Did either of you put a lost and found ad in the paper?"

"No!" Ammy flared.

"Um, yes," Simon said, "but not about a car. We found something small." He held his thumb and forefinger an inch apart.

"We found something small, Vern," Celeste told the phone. "Oh — I see. No, smaller than that. Sorry."

She hung up and dumped her flyers on the kitchen table. "It was small, he said. A Volkswagen. Now, what's this valuable thing you found?"

After Simon finished explaining, and Ammy dug the ring out of her pocket and handed it over, Celeste looked at it from all sides, rubbed the stone with her thumbnail, and handed it back. "Unusual," she said.

"Valuable? Who knows? But you're doing the right thing."

She made a pot of orange-flavoured tea for the three of them, and then went back down to Boomer Heaven, which was closed for New Year's Day — a chance to catch up on work for tomorrow's sale, she said.

Simon tried to convince Ammy that the ad was not a stupid idea. "I mean, that ring may have nothing to do with what happened the first night — the blue light, and the thing that you say happened but you forgot —"

"— that we all forgot, because you were there too —"

"— but suppose it does?"

"If it does, d'you really think whoever owns it is going to phone up and claim it?"

"Well —"

"He'll come crawling in my window in the middle of the night, that's what he'll do!"

"We don't know that he crawls. He probably walks, like any other person."

They answered calls for the next two hours. Most of the callers had lost wallets, or cell phones, or keys, or kittens. Some, like Vern, had elastic ideas about the word "small." About every fourth call was from Ike. "Nothing yet," Simon kept telling him. Mara did not call.

At one o'clock Ammy was propped on the windowsill, brooding out at the blizzard — which was wilder and thicker than ever — and Simon was sitting on a chair by the phone, leafing through a catalogue of robotic airplane models, when the phone rang again. He picked it up.

§

Turning from the window, Amelia saw Simon's head go up. His eyes darted at hers.

"Mara?" She was halfway across the kitchen, hand out, reaching.

He shook his head and covered the receiver with his palm. "I think this is it." He held the receiver towards her and stepped away from the phone. She wondered why he didn't want to take the call himself. Would've expected him to hog it.

"Hello?"

There was a hissing sound on the line. Then a voice: "You have what is mine." Then the hissing sound again.

Amelia's arms went all gooseflesh under her sweater. Funny voice. A voice with no colours in it, no ups and downs, each word like a separate little bar of lead. "Uh … can you describe it, please?" She tried to catch Simon's eye. He was rummaging in a drawer.

"It is a ring." A pause, and that hissing again. "It has a stone." *Hiss…*

What's that sound? Amelia wondered.

"The stone is marked." *Hiss…*

Amelia rubbed a chilled arm with the hand that wasn't holding the phone. "Ah — it — yeah. Uh…"

Simon waved to get her attention. He had pushed aside the clutter on the fridge door and was writing something on the white surface with black marker.

"Uh — y-you said the stone is marked," she said as Simon continued to write. "What mark?"

Hisss… "The eye of wisdom. The claw of strength."

"Well, that … that could be it." Her stomach felt like she'd swallowed cement. "But there could be more than one ring like that," she said, though she doubted it. "What colour is it?"

The line went *hiss… hiss…* She thought: *That's his breathing*. Her heart thumped.

"Bone." *Hisss…*

"Ah!" She nearly laughed. "Sorry, that's not —"

"And blood."

"Oh…"

Simon poked her in the shoulder. She looked at the fridge door. "TELL HIM TO MEET YOU. TOWN HALL SQUARE BY SKATING RINK," it said.

"Uh … we … I…. Uh, meet me in the town hall square. By the skating rink."

Hiss… "Yesss." *Hiss…* "Now." The line went dead.

CHAPTER SIXTEEN
EYES LIKE DIAMONDS

Amelia dropped the receiver on the floor with a clatter and sat down hard in the chair. "Now. He wants me to meet him now."

Simon scooped up the receiver, tapped the hook switch, and dialed again. "Ike? Guess what?"

Amelia took a minute to get her breath. It felt like she'd hardly been breathing, trying not to make a noise: hiding like a rabbit from a snake.

"See you downstairs," Simon said into the phone. He hung up and looked at Amelia.

"I'm scared." She didn't feel the least bit embarrassed about saying it.

"He scared me too. That's why we're bringing Ike and Celeste."

"Why would we —" she began hotly. Then changed her mind. As she headed to the coat closet and started pulling on layers, she said, "Well, okay. After all, we don't know what this guy is. He could be a child molester or a con man or something."

But Celeste wasn't in the store. "Left for Elora fifteen minutes ago, to meet a seller," her helper said. "She'll be back in an hour or so."

"We can't wait an hour," Simon said. "He'll be gone by then."

Ike fell into step with them as they came out of Boomer Heaven. The front of his parka bulged. "Camera," he explained. "Zoom lens. Got to keep it warm."

"Wait a minute," Amelia said breathlessly. They were slogging through ten inches of snow. "Wait — what are we going to do? I can't just hand the ring over!"

"No, you should stall him — as long as you can," Ike panted. "So I can get a good shot!"

"But I don't" — she gasped — "don't want to give it back."

And then it was too late. They reached the corner of Barth's Drugstore, next to the town hall square. Ike stopped, and Simon and Amelia walked out into the square.

"What about Ike?" she asked.

"We can't let him see Ike with us, or he'll never get the shot."

The space in front of the town hall was white and wild. Snow devils eddied as high as the roofs. The only building around the square that showed any sign of life was the doughnut shop on the far side. The square was deserted except for the two of them and a dark figure that sat at one of the concrete chess tables beside the skating rink. Amelia stopped.

"I see him," Simon said. "Don't be scared, I'm with you." His voice trembled. Amelia let the "Don't be scared" remark pass. She didn't think she could speak.

The man turned his head and watched them come. Amelia shaped her mouth into what she hoped was a confident smile. From here he looked nothing like his voice. She wasn't sure what she'd expected, but it wasn't this.

She stopped behind the chair on the near side of the chess table, just beyond arm's reach.

"Sit." His voice was deep and husky, but there was no hissing.

"No, thank you," Amelia said.

"I can pay." He opened his hand and a toonie slid into the snow on the table.

Amelia blinked at it. "Pay?" Her mind was too busy with the man's looks to pay attention to what he was saying.

"For the ad," Simon muttered behind her. "If confirmed, the owner pays for the ad."

"You have what is mine," the man said.

"Uh … yes." Her right hand clenched and she resisted the urge to put it behind her back. The ring nestled warm in her palm. *Strong*, it told her. *Strong and fearless.*

He was strangely dressed. The clothes were not strange in themselves; in fact, he was better dressed than anybody she had seen in Dunstone yet. He wore a dark grey suit with a waistcoat of iridescent satin, grey rippling into green and purple when it moved, like a grackle's head. A silky, dusk purple tie was tucked into the waistcoat and a silver chain looped across it. She glanced down. Glossy black leather shoes showed at the bottoms of knife-creased trouser legs.

And that was all. No overcoat, no scarf, no hat, no gloves, no galoshes. Snow settled in heaps on his shoulders and the wind tore his hair. And yet he didn't look cold.

Dark hair, glossy, with the same iridescence as the waistcoat. Pale face with gaunt bones. Long, slightly smiling mouth. Eyes…

Amelia didn't want to look at his eyes. That would be getting too close. But she made herself do it. The eyes, under thick black eyebrows, were large and pale grey. She looked away again quickly. Most people would say it was a good face, she thought. Not handsome, but kind of … well, noble, in a worn sort of way. She put up a hand and rubbed her eyes. Her head hurt.

"You may sit without fear," he said. "I will not eat you." His accent sounded only a little foreign. Less than at first. That worried her.

"N-no, thanks." Amelia wondered where Ike was and if he'd got his picture yet. "I ... I have to ask one more question. To be sure." She'd seen him before. Where?

"Then ask."

"This, uh, ring you lost. What size is the band?"

"The same size as the ... dial..." His eyes searched her face. Pain walked in her head. She flinched. "... of the ... watch ... on the table beside your bed."

"How would you know that?"

Simon sidled closer. "Ike needs more time," he breathed in her ear.

"There's only one way you could know. You were the thing at my window." Her voice trembled. "You're the Assassin."

The corners of his mouth curled up. "And the ring in your glove is mine."

"I — ah —" How did he know it was in her glove? She took a step back. Her fist clenched tighter.

Simon grabbed her arm. "'Nother sec," he murmured.

"I have no quarrel with you or your friends. You are perfectly safe."

His eyes were tight to her face. It felt like some-thing was walking around on the inside surface of her skull. Digging at her brain with a spade. "What are you doing?"

"Reading you. Learning." His white teeth showed. "You are so open, you people. You don't guard your thoughts at all."

"You're reading my *mind*?"

"Of course. A moment ago you were thinking quite loudly, 'If he's the Assassin he mustn't get the ring. It must be something he needs to hurt Mara. I can't let him hurt Mara.'" He smiled up at her. *Such a nice, warm smile,* she thought wildly.

"The way you talk has changed," Simon said sud-denly. "You've been skimming it off Ammy's mind, haven't you? Is that how Mara learned? By reading our minds?"

"No!" Amelia snapped. "Mara would never do a thing like that to me."

The Assassin laughed at her. "Wouldn't she? Ask her. And while you're at it, see if she'll tell you who she is, and what she is. Ask her why she was exiled, and what was her crime. Perhaps you'll think again before you help such a one as Marathynarradin. And now — the ring, if you please!"

Trying to think of nothing at all, Amelia took the first step away. The Assassin leaped straight over the table at her. She shrieked and crashed flat in the snow. A weight squashed all the breath out of her lungs. She stared up into eyes like diamonds, too bright. She shrieked again. Sharp things tore at her right glove. She hit out with her left fist and kept on shrieking.

Then there were shouts, and chunks of snow hit her in the face, and the weight suddenly lifted. She sat up dizzily. Simon was scrambling to his feet. His left side was coated with snow. Another snowball flew past her, followed by Ike and a fat, grey-haired man wearing a white apron over a red shirt. She looked around for the Assassin. He was gone.

"So much for him," said the man, wiping wet hands on his apron. "You all right?" He held out a hand and pulled Amelia to her feet.

"Y-yeah, thanks. Just — just shaky."

"You watch who you talk to after this, eh? Don't get taken in by how nice they dress."

"I — I won't," Amelia said.

"I'll tell the police to keep their eyes open for this character. Shows you can't tell a book by its cover, eh?"

"Thanks, Bruce," Ike said. The man waved and walked back to the doughnut shop. Ike held out a honey-glazed cruller with one bite out of it. Amelia shook her head. Her stomach churned.

"Did he get it?" Simon asked her.

"No. But…" She held up her right fist. White fleece poked up out of four parallel slashes in the black leather. The back of the glove looked like someone had taken a razor to it.

Ike made a choked sound. Simon said, "I didn't see a knife."

"No," Amelia said. "He didn't have a knife."

CHAPTER SEVENTEEN
IN A HIGH PLACE

The ruined glove lay on the table between them. Ammy touched it with her fingertip. "I'm sorry. It was your dad's."

"Never mind," Simon said. "It kept you from getting cut."

He was just starting to feel warm again, and Ammy's hands had almost stopped shaking. At least, she could hold a drink without sloshing it. They'd been in the doughnut shop twenty minutes. Bruce had brought them mugs of hot chocolate and half a dozen doughnuts, all kinds. "On the house," he said. "Today's a writeoff anyways."

They sat at a table close to the kitchen, away from the window. The square outside still whirled with snow. Simon kept his eye on the window, but nobody moved out there.

Ike had not been able to get a photo: too much snow in the air. "I wish I had. Funny, when I see that" — he touched the glove — "I think of those footprints. You know, with the pointy crampons. Did you get a good look at his feet?"

"Shoes," Simon said. "Ordinary shoes."

"You talked to him a lot. Who is he, anyway? What does he want?"

"Um…" Simon looked at Ammy.

She shook her head. "We promised!"

"He already knows some of it. Besides, he could help find Mara."

"Maybe he won't want to, when he knows."

"Hey, I'm here!" Ike waved his chocolate-glazed between them. "Talk to *me*!"

"Ammy?"

"Oh … all right!"

And so Simon told the whole story. Everything he knew for sure, anyway. Not all his fears and guesses. When he finished Ike said, "Huh," and put down the last doughnut half-eaten. "Y'know, there's an obvious explanation for all this."

"Ike," Simon began patiently.

"UFO, right?" Ike looked even perkier than usual. "I mean, it fits so well. They both came here on a transporter beam — that was the blue light in the cave. And your Mara, she obviously has super mind powers. She's an alien. They both are."

"Ike," Ammy tried.

"Only, that would be a story. Not real." Ike looked from face to face. "And this is real. Isn't it? You're not fooling me. It's not a game."

Ammy nodded. So did Simon.

"So, so, who ... what..." Ike swallowed.

"Ike, listen." Ammy leaned over the table and spoke quietly, so Bruce wouldn't hear. "You're closer than you think. The Assassin isn't human. He looked human for a bit. But then he started to change. We think maybe he comes from somewhere else. Not Earth."

They all looked at the glove, with its parallel slashes.

"And ... and Mara," Ike said unsteadily. "Can she change too?"

"She's not like him!" Ammy sat back. "She's a person like us! No matter where she comes from."

"What did he say?" Simon put in. "'See if she'll tell you who she is, and *what* she is. And what her crime was.'"

"But he's the enemy. Why should we listen to him?"

"Ammy, how can we be sure who's the enemy? Maybe there is no enemy."

"Or maybe they both are," Ike said.

"Well, look!" She pointed at the glove. "He would

have done that to my hand. But Mara, last night — she was trying to protect me. So, what do *you* think?" She pushed back her chair. "Snow's stopping."

Simon caught up with her at the door and followed her out. "Where are you going?"

"To find her. To give her the ring. Like he said — if he wants it, then it could be something she needs."

"We don't even know where to start looking!"

"Might as well start at the apartment," Ike said. He grinned nervously when they both turned around and looked at him.

"You don't have to be mixed up in this," Simon said. "You could go home."

"And miss the fun?"

"Ike, it's not —"

"Not a game. I know. I'm in!"

They went back to the Hammer Block, but Mara wasn't on the roof or in apartment 3A. It was close to three o'clock, and the sunlight was long and slanting, when Simon said, "She'd be lying low somewhere, if she's hurt."

"Uh-uh." Ammy shook her head. "She'd find somewhere high. She really likes being in a high place."

"Of course! More strategic," Ike said. "Where's the last place you saw her?"

"That park on the north side of town, last night."

"Founders Park," Simon said. He looked at Ike

and Ike looked at him and they said in unison, "Founders Tower."

§

It stood on a ridge above the town, a mile east of where Ammy had lost Mara the night before: a tower built of rough stones, fifty feet high, with a cone-shaped shingled roof.

"It was one of those heritage projects," Simon told Ammy. "It marks where the first settlers in the county started farming. People picnic here in the summer. They go up the tower for the view."

"But it's locked in winter," Ike said. "Supposed to be, anyway."

An iron gate blocked the arched opening at the base of the tower, but the chain that normally stretched across it hung loose at one side. Ike fished in the snow and held up a bent iron staple with some bolts dangling from it. "That was the piece the chain looped through."

Ammy pulled the gate open. She stepped inside, and Simon followed her, with Ike crowding in behind. After the brilliance of the sun and snow, it was dark in here. Narrow stone steps spiralled upward into the gloom. Not much light got in through the slits in the thick walls.

"Mara!" Ammy called. No answer. "Mara! Are you up there? It's me, Amelia!"

Still no answer, except a sighing sound that might have been the wind whistling through the slits in the walls. "Either she's not there —" Ike began.

"Or she's hurt." Ammy started up the stairs, sliding both hands up the curving walls. There was no hand rail. Simon kept close behind her.

They climbed out at the top onto a platform with a chest-high stone parapet all around and wide spaces between the arches that held up the roof. Snow had drifted in and piled up at one side against the parapet. There was nothing else to see.

Then the snowdrift moved. Ammy said "Oh!" and dropped to her knees beside it. "Mara!" The snow fell away in big crusty sections. Mara sat up, stretched, and yawned like a cat.

"Mara, what happened? Are you all right?"

"We fight. I don't win, I don't lose. I am a little burned."

"Burned!"

"Yes. He is good, that one. Or else it would be me that burns him up! But look, the firebird coat — I keep her safe." She picked up a neatly folded bundle by her side and shook it out to show off the sequined coat. "I take off all the clothes you give me before I fight, of course."

Ike gasped. "You mean you —"

Mara struggled up, shedding clumps of snow. "What is that?"

Ammy grabbed her arm while Simon backed away, with Ike behind him. He'd forgotten how tall she was. Her head dipped at Ammy like a snake, her teeth gleamed. "You promised! You broke your promise!"

"No! Yes! But we had to! This is Ike — he's a friend!" Ammy kept a grip on her arm. "He — he saved me from the Assassin!"

Mara went very still. She sniffed at Ammy's jacket. "Yes, I smell him on you. Tell." She leaned against the parapet and slowly slid down it. *She can't stand up*, Simon thought. "You two." She pointed at Simon and Ike. "Sit. You must not be higher than me."

"Why —" Ike began, but Simon shushed him. Ammy described their meeting with the Assassin and how it ended. Then she pulled off her torn right glove and held out her hand. "This was what he wanted, but he didn't get it. Is it yours?"

"Yes!" Mara reached for the ruby ring, then dropped her hand. "You have kept it well. You are a true friend, Amelia. And you, Simon. And you, Ike. He could do great harm to me with this."

"Um…" Simon cleared his throat. "Does this mean you'll be going home soon?"

Ike leaned forward. "And by the way, where is home, exactly?"

"Leave her alone!" Ammy flared. "She'll go when

she's ready!" She held out the ring again. "Why don't you take it?"

"Because you may need it." Mara narrowed her eyes at Simon. "Soon you will see me no more. That will please you."

"Are you reading my mind?"

She grinned with all her teeth. "No need. Your face says it."

"I just think," he said carefully, "that we'll all be better off when you're back in your own world. That's if you can get back. He said you were exiled."

"Simon," Ammy said warningly.

"What did you do, to get kicked out? Did you steal that ring?"

"Simon!"

"Steal?" Mara's head rose. "I?" She seemed to get bigger, in that way she had when she was angry. The shadows darkened and spread around her like wings. How did she do that?

Behind him, Ike eased towards the top of the stairs. Simon kept his eyes fixed on Mara, glittery-eyed in her cloak of shadows. If only Ammy wasn't right next to her. It would be hard to grab her away if Mara moved suddenly.

Mara sighed and sank back, and the shadows ebbed. "Don't fear." She touched Ammy's arm. "He pleases me. He is brave." She looked at Simon. "The ring is old. It is from my ... old ones, grandmothers, far back in time. Amelia?"

"Ancestors?"

"Yes, good. It stays with the chief of my people."

"Then you did..." Simon began.

Mara growled in her throat. "It is mine! Bone of my bone, blood of my blood. Mine!"

The only noise was the wind, wuffling past their ears.

"You mean," Ammy said, "*you* are the chief of your people."

"Since seven days."

Ammy let out a little whoop and sat back. "I'm not surprised! It all fits!"

Ike said, "Seven days? What happened seven days ago?"

"My grandmother died. She was chief. I am ... one who follows. Who is chosen. Amelia?"

"Heir," Ammy supplied. "You're the heir. And your brother — don't tell me — he stole the crown!"

"Crown? There is no crown."

"I mean, he..."

"Staged a coup," Ike said. "A takeover."

Mara blinked at him. "First, he challenge. That is fair. We fight before the people. I win, of course — the ancestors are with me, not with him. But then I make a mistake." She smiled and shook her head. "I did not want to show a small spirit. So I let him live."

"Of course!" Ammy sat back. "And he wasn't grateful?"

"He hated me for it. It made him less. So he bowed his neck and he waited, and then he sent his followers to catch me alone. They were many." She turned her head away. "I could not fight."

"So you came here. And he sent the Assassin to make sure you wouldn't come back." Ammy looked at the ring in her hand. "And to get this, I guess."

"Without it even his own followers will say he brings bad blood." Mara leaned back against the parapet. "When I go back I must be ready to fight. I go as soon as I am strong."

Ammy kneeled forward. "We have to get you to a doctor!"

"Doctor: this is healer? No. I heal myself."

"But —"

"If you bring a doctor I am gone."

"At least let us get you somewhere warm."

"No. I like this place. I am warm enough. And the Assassin will not attack here; he is not stupid. But maybe you can help."

"Anything." Ammy sat down cross-legged beside her.

"There is a thing I need now. If I were strong I would get it."

"What, some kind of weapon?" Ike asked, from behind Simon's shoulder.

"No, a thing to see and hear. To know what happens in my country."

"A TV?" Ammy guessed.

"You would call it a book. The Book of Lands. A thing the elders found long ago."

"Book of Lands," Ammy repeated. "Really? Well, how do we get it?"

"Listen close." Mara leaned forward. "They keep it in a safe place, but you can go there. The ring will open the door. If you do what I say, there is no danger."

CHAPTER EIGHTEEN
PASSAGE

It was 4:50 by Simon's watch and the sun was shining dead straight along the gorge when they stood together on the ledge in front of the cave.

"There's a lot about this that bothers me," Simon said. "There's too much she hasn't told us. Like, where exactly this passage goes, and why we have to come straight back."

"Maybe she isn't hiding anything," Ammy said. "Maybe she isn't all that sure of how it works, herself."

"Funny how that doesn't make me feel any better." Ike dug two flashlights out of his pack — heavy, powerful ones, this time — and handed one to Simon.

Simon held his flashlight up like a weapon. "Okay, in we go!"

"Aren't you scared?" Ike demanded.

"You kidding? 'Course I am — just like you."

"I'm not." Ammy's voice trembled only a little more than her hands. "Mara said it won't be dangerous, and I trust her."

Duck under the low place, crawl and crawl, stand up. There they were. Two bright flashlight beams lit up the cave. "So, where is it?" Ike demanded. "I don't see it."

"You weren't listening." Ammy faced the wall with the graffiti on it. "We won't see it at first," she said rapidly. "Not till I unlock it. I have to use the ring. It's like a key. Like I did the last time, accidentally. When I did … this."

She took off her glove and held out the ring towards the rough stone face. "Only, last time, the ring was inside my glove. It didn't actually touch."

She touched the ruby to the grey stone. The only sound was Ike unzipping his camera case. Nothing happened to the wall. Ammy let out her breath and lowered her arm.

Simon let his breath out, too. "Well," he began. "That's…"

Something was happening to the wall.

Blue light bled through the bright yellow of the flashlight beams. A tall rectangle of blue light with a curved top. With twining shapes like tree roots all over it, only glassy — no, jewel-like — no, clear and deep as the evening sky.

Ike's flashlight crashed to the floor. His camera buzzed and clicked.

Simon got a good grip on his own flashlight and, remembering that they'd planned to keep track of the time, looked at his watch: 4:52.

Ammy stood absolutely still. The door shone before them, solid, beautiful. And closed. She raised her arm again and touched the ring to the door. It flared electric blue. When Simon could pry his eyes open again, the door was gone and an arched tunnel of brilliant blue light stretched away in front of him. The far end was lost in dazzle.

Ammy grabbed a breath and looked at him. He couldn't speak. *Go in there? I can't!*

"I always said I wanted to go places." She laughed shakily.

"I never did, specially, but…" *But if I don't go in, I'll spend the rest of my life wondering…*

"Yes," Ammy croaked. She grabbed his free hand and stepped forward. Ike yelped and grabbed his other sleeve. They walked forward side by side. Blue light curved around them and under them. Like walking in sky. Simon didn't dare look down.

A high, sweet humming made his ears tingle. "It's singing," Ammy whispered.

"It's something to do with those … what are they?" Lines of light branched around the tunnel, around and under, always moving. Dart, flicker, vanish, like snakes' tongues — he wished he hadn't thought that — or like electricity, arcing from point to point. The singing sounded electric.

As they walked the sound rose higher, sweeter, more piercing. The tunnel became a deeper, richer blue. Blue as the depths of the sea, blue as dusk. There was no up or down to it. Simon wasn't walking now, he was sliding. Sliding on his feet down an endless curve of twilight sky.

He heard Ammy yell but he couldn't feel her hand. He heard Ike yell, and somebody else yell, and...

And then they were lying in a tangled heap someplace where the light was not blue. The singing faded to a sigh and then to nothing.

Ike groaned. "I feel like some of me got left behind."

"Not your feet, anyway," Ammy snapped. "Get them off my stomach!"

Simon rolled painfully off the debris of his flashlight, stood up and looked around. Good thing it wasn't dark here. The blue door stood behind them, but it wasn't glassy and shining. It looked painted on the wall. Not a stony cave wall. A wall that was smooth and reddish brown, like clay tile.

"Where are we?" Ike was up and aiming his camera. He took a picture of the painted-on door, then held up his camera. "Darn! It's stopped working! Must've been that tunnel." He shuddered.

"Felt like riding a bolt of lightning," Simon agreed. He looked at his watch. The digital display was blank. He held out his wrist to Ike, who checked his own watch and nodded.

"Temporal distortion effect," Ike said.

"That's just words." Ammy unzipped her jacket. Simon did the same. It was warm here, or at least not cold. "You don't have a clue what's going on," she added briskly. "Now, where's that book? Mara said we'd see it right away. Take the book and get out fast, she said. Don't hang around."

They were standing in a triangular space with walls stretching away from them left and right. About twelve paces away the ends of six rows of shelves began, all of them the same smooth reddish brown as the walls. Simon moved his head and squinted. The shelves radiated away in all directions. Something wrong with this. He looked again. Shook his head.

"This'll give me a headache."

"It's already given me a headache." Ammy rubbed her forehead.

"Now we know for sure." Ike gripped his camera case. "We aren't in Ontario any more."

"Then where are we?" Ammy's lips whitened.

"No clue. But that's nothing to be scared of," Simon said past the coldness in his chest. "We know the way back."

She forced a grin. "Sure. Mara wouldn't be scared. So I won't be."

A tall, narrow table stood in the middle of the triangular space. It looked like the lectern in the Dunstone Public Library that held the big Oxford Dictionary. Maybe it *was* a lectern, because a book was on it. "This must be it." Ammy picked up the book, using both hands. "Oof. Heavy!" It was about a foot tall and eight inches wide and a good two inches thick, and it was bound in dark green leather in a reptile pattern.

"Is that snakeskin?" Simon touched it. "What's that on the front?"

A shape was pressed into the centre of the cover. It looked like an eye, oval with two pointed ends. A line curved out from each end.

"It's the same symbol as on the ring. Guess that proves this is Mara's book." Ammy braced it against her hip. "Right, we've got it, let's go! Ike!"

Ike had got over being scared. He was in among the shelves. "What a place!" he called. "Look at all this stuff!"

"Mara said not to go farther!"

"Probably thought we'd get lost," Ike called back. "We won't. Look — I can't travel through a dimensional gate and then just turn around and go back!"

"Me neither," Simon said.

"Well...." She shrugged one shoulder. "There's nothing here but us. We'll just have a little look."

They followed Ike along an aisle between two rows of shelving. On each side were hundreds of books in bindings of all colours and materials, including some bound in what looked like metal or glass. Some had writing on the spines in gold or black or shining colours. The writing was not in any language Simon recognized. The characters were strange.

"This place is huge!" Ike pointed upward. The shelves rose until they faded into the shadows high above. The ceiling, if there was one, was invisible in the dark.

In between the books were jars and bottles and boxes. Simon stopped to brush the dust off a quart-sized jar and found himself looking through the glass into a hideous little face. He jumped when the thing — it looked like a rat with no hair or tail — blinked at him. "Look at this!"

It was floating in a cloudy liquid, like a science exhibit. "How can it be alive in there?" Ike put his nose close to the jar. "I wonder if we should let it out." He reached toward the lid, and the animal opened jaws lined with teeth like skewers and snapped at his hand. The jar rocked. He backed off. "I don't think so."

They walked and walked. They passed books the size of tables and books no bigger than Simon's thumb. And not just books.

"Look!" Ammy pointed out a small silver box with scenes of marching men etched in its sides: men in armour and cone-shaped helmets, with spears on their shoulders and banners flying over their heads. "Isn't this neat!" She reached to lift the lid.

"I wouldn't," Simon began.

As soon as Ammy touched it, the lid flew up and hundreds of squeaking mice poured out and scattered. All three of them yelped and jumped back. In seconds the mice were all gone.

Ike craned his neck to see into the box without touching it. "How could all those mice have been in there?"

"Maybe they weren't really mice," Simon said. "Or maybe that wasn't just a box. Did you see? Some of them were holding little sticks in their teeth."

"What kind of a place is this, anyway?"

"Maybe it's a kind of weird museum," Ammy said. "Mm, look at this!"

On a wooden stand sat a cap made of overlapping feathers in the blue-purple-gold of a peacock's tail. Simon bent close, not daring to touch. A faint twittering sound came from it. He wondered what it was for.

"Hey, this is cool." Ike was squinting through a brass tube that looked like a telescope. "You can see another country through here. Really! It's summer there. There's hills and trees and things, and the trees are moving — like the wind is blowing — and, hey, there's some guy lying in that grass under the trees, and he's — oh, neat, I think he sees me!" Ike lowered the tube to beam at Simon.

"Careful!" Simon reached for the tube, but Ike swung it away and put his eye back to the lens. "He definitely sees me — he's pointing something — *ah*!" A flash lit up Ike's cheek, and the tube jumped in his hand. He dropped it back onto the shelf.

"Told you," Simon said. "Ammy, did you see that?"

She didn't answer. When Simon looked back at her, she was reading that book of Mara's. She had it open and propped on a shelf, and her fingers were resting on a blue square. There was nothing else on the page.

"Ammy?"

She blinked once, slowly. Otherwise, she didn't move.

CHAPTER NINETEEN
INTO THE DEPTHS

So, what's in this book of Mara's? Amelia wondered. Simon and Ike were playing with that brass tube, so she set the book down on an empty shelf, opened it, and flipped through. The paper was thick and stiff. Funny, there was no print, just squares of colour — one big square on each right-hand page. All different. Shadowy purple, foggy grey, fiery red, canary yellow, blue-black with glints like stars. And dozens more.

Here was a square of blue-green. Her hand stopped. "Oh...." She had never seen such a beautiful colour, so deep and rich, like a lake cupped between mountains. She touched it with her fingertips and — yes, it had depth. It felt wet. It actually was...

Water.

Amelia was no longer looking at the blue-green square. She was in it. Her mouth opened in a yell, but instead of choking, she found she was breathing the water like air.

She forgot to be terrified. The colour was so beautiful. Floating in it was like flying. Almost like her flying dreams, except this was not hot and red but all cool and blue and serene. Below, instead of sharp-edged pinnacles, were soft, feathery plants that waved gracefully between and around smooth rocks.

One of the rocks was tall and straight, with four sides. It was probably ten feet tall, and was clearly not natural. It looked like a war memorial or the kind of thing they put under a statue, only there was no statue.

Above her, like a window, floated a bright, white square. Amelia noticed it, then forgot it. It didn't look important.

Something stirred in the blueness ahead. It became a shadow that grew solid, until she could see it was a person. A boy. His body was thin and bluish white, and no bigger than hers. He undulated through the blueness like an otter, and the weedy green tatters of his clothing undulated with him. She bobbed comfortably and watched him approach.

She thought: *This must be a dream. If it were real I'd be afraid.*

The boy floated in the blueness in front of her. His eyes were the blue-violet colour of chicory, and huge.

Who are you? he mouthed, and a moment later his voice came to her, slow and echoing. "Who are you?"

"I'm Amelia. Amelia Hammer. Who are —"

"You are not one of us. Are you one of the Urdar?"

"Urdar? What's that?"

"Urdar. The Wise Ones." His eyes turned a stormy dark purple. "That's what they call themselves."

"What do you call them?" Amelia asked, to soothe him. It didn't help.

"The destroyers! The enemy! This was our world. Then they came from outside and drove us into the deeps of the sea. And even here they come, leaving their mark." He stabbed an angry finger at the tall stone pillar. "Claiming the last of what is ours for their own!"

"I didn't know that. It's very interesting. But I still don't know who —"

He drifted backward and his eyes narrowed. "But you must know!"

"I'm a stranger," she explained. "I'm new here."

"You could be one of them. They are never what they seem. They steal other people's shapes."

"I'm not one of them, I swear it!" But he was swimming backwards now, keeping his chicory eyes fixed on her. "Don't go!" she called.

He flipped and darted around the tall stone and was gone. Amelia started to swim after him, then back-paddled to stop herself. She stared at the flat front of the stone, where a shape was carved. An eye shape with curved lines coming from the ends. Same as on the cover of the book and on the ring.

Leaving their mark? Was that what he meant?

But something was wrong. It was getting hard to see. The blue-green cooled to blue-purple, then to indigo. The water was icy. Amelia tried to swim up towards the white square. It looked small and far away now. And she was so cold. And it was so hard to move her arms and legs. And it was getting hard to breathe the blueness. Her lungs hurt.

I'm drowning!

Her vision darkened. Just as the darkness became inky, a giant hand reached down from the white square, a hand as big as her whole body. It gleamed bluish white in the gloom. It grabbed her arm and hauled her up into the light.

§

"What's the matter with her?" Ike asked.

"Don't know. Ammy!"

She stood there absorbed in her book, but she wasn't turning pages. Simon gave her arm a shake and she straightened up with a gasp. She slammed the book shut and leaned on it, panting. Simon looked at her, worried.

"What's wrong?"

"This book. You'll never believe — It takes you places —"

"Then you better not open it again."

"Think I'm crazy?" She told them about the underwater boy and his story of the Urdar. "And guess what I saw down there? A stone sort of monument, with this on it!" She tapped the sign on the cover of the book. "Exactly the same thing!"

"Then you were somewhere in Mara's country, I guess," Simon said.

"Urdar, eh?" Ike said. "'Steal other people's shapes.' What are they, body snatchers?"

"They sound like bad news," Simon said.

"But the boy said" — Ammy tapped the book again — "he said this was their sign. That means the Urdar are Mara's people. Mara's not like that!"

"The Assassin is, though. Maybe Mara's brother is, too."

"My headache's worse. And we've been here an awful long time." Ammy squinted along the endless row of shelves. "We should get back."

Simon had a disturbing idea. "Your headache. Like when the Assassin was reading your mind?" He looked around uneasily.

"No. This is like my head's breaking into pieces and crashing back together again." She squeezed her eyes shut. "I think I'm starting to remember something about that first night. I keep getting these images…"

"Maybe going through that passage unscrambled your brain," Ike said. "I wish I could remember. Or maybe not, if it hurts like that."

Simon lifted his head. "Funny!"

"What?" Ike spun around in a panic.

"I can smell fresh air." A tiny breeze lifted a strand of Simon's hair. "There must be a way out of here. Forwards, I mean, not backwards."

Ammy sniffed. "I wonder what we'd find outside?"

"Let's follow the fresh air and find out where it comes from."

"But Mara warned us," Ike began. "Still, we haven't seen anything to be scared of yet. Not even a librarian, or whoever would be in charge here."

"I vote we explore." Simon's hand shot up. "Cautiously."

"I vote the same," Ammy said.

Ike hesitated, then nodded. "Okay. Cautiously."

They followed the scent of fresh air between the towering shelves. Every time they came to a gap between the shelves on the left, they stepped through.

"See? We can't get lost," Simon said. "We're always turning left."

A few paces farther on they came to a gap twice as wide as any of the others. They stepped through, Simon leading, and found a clear space about twenty paces wide. And then a reddish brown wall. In the wall was an archway, with stairs leading down into darkness. Standing at the top they could just make out a landing, and below that more steps disappearing down to the right.

"What's down there?" Simon wondered aloud.

"Sh!" Ammy breathed. "We don't know *who's* down there."

Ike stepped back a pace. "Wonder if my dad's worried yet."

"It can't be that late," Simon said. "We haven't been here all that long."

"I've lost track." Ike took a shaky breath. "Suppose we go back and, like, centuries have passed?"

A river of cool air flowed up the stairs. It carried an earthy, rocky, grassy, unmistakably outdoorsy smell. "I wonder if we could see the stars out there." Simon took a step down. "If we could, maybe we could tell where we are."

"They would look different, wouldn't they?" Ammy said. "Strange stars. Or if it's day, a strange sun." She stepped down beside him.

"A new world. Maybe a different universe." Simon's heart thumped. He exchanged a scared, excited look with Ammy and they took the next step together.

"Um, I don't think..." said Ike, from the top of the stairs.

"C'mon, Ike!" Simon called. "You'll kick yourself for the rest of your life if you don't."

"Sh! Listen!"

Halfway down the flight, they stood still and listened. Below the landing, where they couldn't see, someone was climbing the stairs towards them.

Simon opened his mouth to call out, then closed it again. There was something in the sounds that he didn't like. Whatever was climbing the stairs was heavy and had feet with long nails. It was climbing carefully, as if not to be heard, but its nails clicked on the hard surface of the stairs.

Ammy said nothing, but she gathered a handful of Simon's jacket at the shoulder and tugged. He followed her silently back up the stairs and across the bare space and through the gap in the shelves. Ike was well ahead of them.

At first they tiptoed. But after a few minutes Simon realized there was no use trying to be quiet. The newcomer (the librarian? the door guard?) knew they were here and it (he? she?) was following them. It was walking even more quietly than they were, but it couldn't help making the floor tremble. Glass jars tinkled together on the shelves.

"Better speed up," Simon murmured.

They started off walking fast, but soon they were running — Ike in the lead, then Ammy, clutching the book to her chest, then Simon. Not far behind, a row of books crashed to the ground. The newcomer must be running too, its body scraping the shelves on both sides.

They leaped through a gap one after the other and passed the silver box with the open lid. "We're close!" Ike gasped.

Simon looked ahead and saw the jar with the ferocious little specimen inside. At the same moment feet with hard nails scrabbled the floor behind and he knew it had squeezed through the gap and seen them.

He didn't look back. No time. "Ammy! Get the door open!" As he reached the jar he slowed down half a second to grab it in both hands.

Ammy and Ike burst from the row of shelves and across the bare triangle towards the painted door. Simon saw Ammy reach out with the ring. He tossed the jar backwards over his head.

CHAPTER TWENTY
A CLOUD OF RUBIES

Simon expected a crash and a stink, but instead there was a crunch and something made a noise like the gears of a car grinding together. The footsteps behind him lost their galloping rhythm.

The door on the wall came to life, glowed, and flared. Ike looked back. "Simon, c'mon!" he yelled. Ammy, beside him, glanced back and froze.

Simon didn't waste his breath shouting. He piled into Ike and Ike barged into Ammy and they fell into the shining blue tunnel in a tangle of arms and legs.

§

Amelia's head was full of blue light. It hurt. She whimpered and tried to open her eyes. Saw rough grey rock. So they were back, safe and sound. Great.

"You okay?" Simon's voice boomed in her ear.

Her head whirled with jagged bits of images broken up by rays of dazzling blue light. A shape was forming out of the jumble. There was something about that shape. She felt she would recognize it if she could just get a good look.

"What's the matter?" Booming voice again.

"Head." She drew up her knees and buried her face on her crossed arms. That shape... Relax. Let it come. *The way it came from the cave mouth, bending low, then rising up, with the blue light streaming out around it like a crown.*

"I'm one big bruise," Simon announced, farther away. "But we're all in one piece, right? Ike?"

"I'm okay. Hey, my watch is working again — 4:53! Yours?"

"The same. Looks like we just picked up where we left off."

And leaped. Across the gorge. No, not leaped. Sailed. Glided.

"I wonder what time it really is?" Simon again.

"Well, there you go." A distant bonging drifted from the cave entrance. "That's the clock in the town hall."

Shining like a cloud of jewels. Rubies, floating overhead. So beautiful. So...

"Two ... three..." They counted together. "Four ... five..." The bonging stopped.

169

"Five o'clock," Ike said. "So, all that took us only eight minutes! That's if this is the same day we started, and not twenty years from now."

"We were in there a lot longer than eight minutes," Simon said. "Ammy? What d'you — um, are you okay?"

Rubies sparkled overhead. Lightning tore at her mind, tore bits of it away. Something thudded to the ground a few feet away.

Amelia opened her eyes. They stood over her like gawkers at a car crash. Simon held the book under one arm. She felt like her heart was being squeezed in half.

She pushed herself up to her knees, then lurched to her feet. Head not so bad now. Now that the picture was complete.

"I'm just wonderful."

Even Ike didn't look as if he believed that, but neither of them disagreed.

Nobody suggested waiting to find out if anything interesting might come out of the cave after them, and nobody dawdled as they climbed down the cliff and slithered among the rocks and ice to the path up to Deacon Street. As Simon climbed out at the top of the path, the last in line, he took a look back along the gorge, where the rocks and ice gleamed pink in the afterglow of sunset. He let out a sigh of relief.

"That was some watchdog," Ike said. "I don't see how anything that big could have chased us between those shelves."

"What kind of thing was it?" Simon asked.

"I had a split-second look, that's all. It was big and the front end was all teeth."

"Only eight minutes." Simon shook his head. "Are we sure it really happened?"

"We have this for proof." Ike tapped the book. "A genuine alien artifact!"

"That's right!" Simon bounced as he walked. "We'll make history! We..." He looked at Amelia. "Oh, right," he said flatly. "We have to take it to Mara. It's hers."

Such a pair of kids, she thought. "Yeah, we better. Because now I know what Mara is."

Her right hand went into her pocket. The ring was there, hard and warm. The pulse in her thumb flickered against the stone. It was like a friend's hand in hers. *Liar.*

§

I'll be cool, Amelia promised herself as she led the way up Founders Tower. *I'll just hand the things over and say, "Fine, you got what you came for, so long, goodbye."*

She half hoped the platform would be deserted when they reached it. But Mara was there, still sitting

171

against the parapet, like she hadn't moved a muscle while they were away risking their lives in another dimension.

"Well, here we are," Amelia said, and was surprised to hear herself sounding so normal.

Mara opened her eyes. "You are not hurt?"

"Like you care?"

Mara's head went up. "You are angry. Why?"

"Why not just rummage in my mind and find out?"

Mara looked at her. In the twilight it was impossible to read her face. Light from somewhere reflected off her eyes and made two glowing green spots in the gloom. *Monster,* Amelia thought. Simon was pulling at her arm. She ignored him.

"You remember," Mara said.

"Yeah, I remember. I know what you are and what you did to me."

"That was…" Mara pulled herself up and leaned against the parapet. Amelia felt a twinge of pity and stifled it. "Accident," Mara finished. "I was afraid."

"Right, like the other night, when you ran off to fight the Assassin, and blasted my mind so I couldn't see what you really looked like!"

"No! I just … made a little light in front, so you not see. I did not want you hurt."

"Oh, yeah?" Amelia laughed. "So that's why you sent us to get that book? We just missed being eaten!

That's what it's all been about, right? You get in my mind and, and make me" — *I won't cry. I won't!* — "do things for you, risk my life to get that — that stupid book. Well, here it is. Take it and go away. Give it to her, Simon."

She turned and groped for the doorway. Where was the darn stair?

"Amelia!" And in her mind, faintly: *Amelia!* She whirled around.

"Get out of my mind! I thought you were — I thought — thought you were my friend. And all the time it was this, wasn't it?" She held out her fist. "You used it to control me."

"That?" Mara straightened up. "It has no power. Only against me."

"You *made* me like you!" Her fingers hurt. She unclenched them. The ruby ring had cut into the skin. She hurled it at Mara, who scooped it out of the air without looking at it.

"I have no words," Mara said in a strange, small voice.

"Right, like you haven't been scraping out my entire vocabulary!"

"I —" Mara began, but Amelia didn't stay to listen. She wondered, later, how she made it to the bottom of the stairs without breaking her neck.

§

Simon let his breath out slowly. He'd been afraid Mara would get really mad and do something violent, but she stayed put the whole time Ammy was ranting and only moved when Ammy crashed down the stairs. Then she oozed back down the parapet and sat.

"So what was all that about?" Ike asked from the top of the stairs, poised for a quick retreat.

Mara said nothing. "I think Ammy remembers what happened, the night of the blue flare," Simon said.

"But we were there too. How come we don't get our memories back?"

"It was not well done," Mara muttered.

Simon decided not to ask any questions. There was something about Mara that made him go on tiptoe. "Um, here's the book." He held it out. She raised her head and looked, then lifted a hand. "Bring. And after, do not touch me."

After what? He wondered. He set it down on the stone floor beside her. Too dark to read, he thought, but she opened the book and turned the pages. Stopped — he couldn't see where — and set her hand down firmly.

For about two minutes there was silence. He'd forgotten how quiet it gets at night in winter. No bird sounds, not even a crow. The wind had fallen. He heard his own breathing, and Ike's, and the faint creak of the tower's timbers down the stairwell. A bitter, burned smell hung in the icy air. He thought it came from the book.

Mara gave herself a shake. She closed the book and pushed it away. "I must go home. My brother is winning. My people are dying." She started to haul herself up the parapet again. Simon found himself at her side, trying to hold her up and push her down simultaneously. She was all thin bones and papery skin and muscles like tree roots.

"You can't go back like that! You'll only get yourself killed!"

She went still. "And then they will truly despair. Yes. You are wise." She slid back down.

"There's a clinic here in Dunstone. Let me bring help."

"No. I heal myself." She pulled up her knees, wrapped her arms around them, and bent her head. Her hair fell like a glinting curtain. "I go home tomorrow," said her muffled voice.

Ike poked Simon in the back. "She's cocooning," he whispered. "Is she through with the book? Can we have it?"

She did look like a cocoon. "Um, Mara? Shouldn't you be someplace warm?"

A green glint opened in the curtain of her hair. "Go away."

"At least put the coat back on!"

Mara growled like a dog. Simon took that as a no. He backed up against Ike, who hissed: "The book!"

"Take the Book of Lands," said the muffled voice. "Take the firebird coat. Go!"

CHAPTER TWENTY-ONE
FOOTPRINTS IN THE SNOW

Ike hung up the phone and stepped out of the booth. "It's okay. My dad says I can stay for supper at your place but I have to be home no later than eight. Can you beat that? I tell him we've discovered another world and he says, 'That's great, kid. Just make sure you're home no later than eight.'"

"Like he'd believe you," Simon said.

"Well, he'll have to now, won't he? Now that we've got proof." Ike touched a corner of the book. Simon was holding it against his chest with both arms wrapped around it.

They'd had to walk west on Hill Street, a block out of their way, to find a phone outside a Mac's Milk store. Even the milk store was closed, and the streets were deserted. At five-thirty on New Year's Day everybody was inside, behind closed curtains and decorated windows, having dinner.

McNairn Street was brighter, with its rows of lit-up store windows. Simon stopped and held the book down where they could both see it. Proof, he thought. A book bound in the green, scaly skin of some other-world creature, with the family emblem of some alien ruler pressed into the cover. "A book of doors," he said. "Or windows?"

"Windows," Ike said.

"Right. Your mind goes through, so you can see, but not your body."

"It must be like a really, really interactive CD."

"Looking into a different world. Maybe a different universe."

"And it's ours!"

Simon took a deep breath. "This is going to change everything."

They exchanged excited grins.

"What really gets me is the time," Ike said. "How long d'you think Ammy was in that underwater place? From all she said, it had to be more than a few minutes, right? But how long was it on our side?"

Simon thought back. "A few seconds. And when we went though the passage? It felt like we wandered around that museum for an hour."

"More."

"Say eighty minutes. But when we got back it was only eight minutes. That's a difference of ten times."

"It must be a quantum thing. We'll experiment."

Simon clutched the book closer. Yes, everything would change once this came out. Not just for him and Ike. For the whole world! Every time he thought of that it made his heart jump.

They crossed McNairn. Not a car in sight. Then, to avoid another detour, they cut through the parking lot next to the school. The glow of the streetlights faded behind them.

Ike laughed suddenly. "We'll be famous. You realize that?"

"That's right. Everybody will want to see it." Simon frowned. "Suppose they try and take it away from us?"

"We'll need help. Somebody who's really big in physics."

"Somebody we can trust."

"If only Carl Sagan was still alive!"

Simon suddenly thought of Mara and Ammy, both of them miserable. It almost seemed unfair he should be so happy. He didn't even care that he'd lost a bit of his memory. That bit about the blue flare, and whatever came after it, that seemed unimportant. Which was odd, when you came to think of it.

"Now, that's funny," Ike said. He pointed. Behind them on the right, the school was a long black silhouette against the glow of streetlights on McNairn. "What's that up there?"

Simon looked. The flat roof of the school changed shape as he watched. Not by much, but something was up there, all right.

Ike kept staring. "There, it moved again."

"Nothing to worry about." Simon pulled at him to get him moving. Whatever it was, it was big. The roof had taken on a strange, humped outline. He didn't like it.

"We ought to get back to the street, where it's bright. But…"

"But we'd have to pass it." Ike blew out a cloud of breath. "Let's get going."

They set off across the school grounds, a sheet of unmarked snow that seemed to stretch forever under the black sky, like an Arctic waste. A row of buildings on Queen Street, on the other side of the grounds, looked far away and tiny.

Simon's legs itched. He wanted to run, but he knew better. Running would open the door to fear. Right now, the door was barely closed.

To their left rose a high fence, with a row of houses behind it. To the right, more open snow and the dark bulk of a church. Not a living soul in sight, except for them. And no sound except their own breathing and the squeak of snow under their boots.

Simon gasped and whipped around.

"What?" Ike yipped.

"Thought I felt something." He started to sweat inside his parka. There was nothing there, of course. Just snow and darkness and the faraway lights.

"Don't get me started." Ike looked back over his shoulder and all around.

Simon laughed. "Nerves!"

"Never thought you had any."

Before they'd taken two more steps, it was there behind them. This time for sure. Simon knew it before he felt the wave of air on his cheek. Ike started to turn.

Then, darkness — sudden, warm, thick — closed down from above. It spread out hugely on both sides and folded them in.

§

When the darkness lifted Simon was lying on his back in the snow. The town hall clock was striking six. He scrambled up, stiff and cold, but ready to run. There was nothing to run from.

Ike struggled to his feet beside him. "You okay?"

"Yeah. You? What was that?"

They were alone. The only sign that anything had happened was the prints of their two bodies, like badly done angels in the snow.

"Simon, the book?"

"It's gone."

As Simon stared down at the ground he noticed something. "Look!" A neat trail of tracks led back through the parking lot. Two sets of boot prints, side by side. His and Ike's. Nobody else's.

"And there." He pointed a shaking finger. Footprints — different ones, not from boots — were spotted around the body marks.

"Like the ones outside the cave," Ike said. "The ones with the crampons."

"But where did they come from? The sky?"

"Well…" Ike pointed. The strange prints led away — one, two, three — then none. The snow beyond that last one lay clean and perfect.

Ike and Simon backed away, turned, and started running. They didn't stop until they reached the Hammer Block.

§

"Ammy? I wish you'd open up." Simon leaned on Ammy's door. He was fed up with trying to talk through it. "I think you're wrong about Mara. I feel like we weren't fair to her."

"She's evil," came the muffled answer. "Look what she can do to people's minds! Remember the mall? The espresso machine eagle?"

"That's just what I mean. If she could do that, she could've made us forget everything we've found out. She could have turned you back into her best friend, like you were at the start. But she didn't."

"She doesn't care. She's got what she wants."

"I think she does care."

"You're wrong."

Getting tired of this.... "Something stole the book. We got mugged, Ike and me."

The door opened. Ammy looked him over. "You okay?"

"Yeah. Ike's dad came in the car and picked him up. But the book —"

"Who cares about the book?" The door slammed.

"And now nobody will believe us," Simon said to himself.

§

Mom, Dad, never mind what I said last time. Please let me come to Peru now!!!! Please! It's urgent! I hate it here and I miss you so much. Hugs and kisses, Amelia.

§

"Ammy? Message from Celeste. She says you should eat."

183

"I'm not hungry."

"There's hot milk in the kitchen. And oatmeal cookies."

"Go away!"

§

Hi Silken. Sounds like you've had a great holiday so far. I wish I was there with you. Everything here is awful. I hate everybody.

CHAPTER TWENTY-TWO
TRUE DREAMS

Amelia thought she would never sleep. Her chest hurt too much. Could this be a heart attack? Could it kill you, this kind of pain?

Not that she cared if Mara was a monster and a liar. Not that she cared one bit.

She dreamed she was soaring over a fantastic city, all points and pinnacles. It was sunset, and the glowing red spires were striped with their own long shadows.

Huge figures sprang from the towers and arrowed up at her. *Climb!* snapped a voice in her head. She beat her wings and surged upward. The pursuers fell away. The city shrank to a carpet of ruby needles.

We are too swift for them, said the voice, smugly. It was familiar, but not...

"That's not my voice."

No, it is me.

"Mara? What are you doing in my dream? Can't I even dream without —"

It is my dream.

"Uh?"

My dream, that you share these three nights. I dream of home.

"Well, that makes a weird kind of sense. Except, why am I sharing your dreams?"

I can dream you the answer. For the Urdar, dreams are truth.

"Go right ahead," Amelia said. "It's only a dream. Nothing that happens here is real."

You are wrong. It is more than real.

The far-below landscape tilted and lifted. The pinnacles swept past, and then a wind-blown plain that glistened red in waves, where the sunset light caught the bending grasses. Ahead rose a long mountain crowned with a ridge of bare cliff, and in the cliff was a gate with stairs leading up between pillars.

Screams broke out behind. They had a gloating sound. The dream sped up. Rows and rows of library shelves whirled past. Behind, more screams, and the clatter and crash of things falling off shelves. Heavy feet battered the floor, closer, closer. Ahead, a blue door. Then a tunnel of blue light. And then…

Terror.

"You? Afraid? I don't believe it."

This world, it was the demon world of the old tales.

"Wait a minute. Demon world?"

Many ages ago the Urdar departed this world. The tales say it was overrun by demons. We took the new world and called it Mythrin, our world. We set a watch on the gate so that none of the demons could pass through.

"Demons. Brother!"

And so I — yes, I — was afraid.

The blue light died, the passage closed. Alone, and safe, but... The demon world was dark and cold and smelled of danger. Minds whispered all around — distant, but unguarded. And one nearer. Something watched from across an abyss. A demon! Two, three demons! They saw! They would call the other demons!

"But that was us! Simon and Ike and me!"

I was afraid. I did a coward thing.

Reached for the watching minds to muddle the memories. Too late, felt a mind like leaves and fog that tore at a touch. Blundered, felt its pain and fear. The two others, close by — touched them too, but gently now, delicately. Sealed off the memory. Shame. No honour in that, harming creatures so weak. Watch them, then. Follow them, leaping through the black skies from roof to roof.

"This is true, isn't it? I think I saw you following us."

Lying is not possible in the dream.

The demon world was strange. The buildings short and fat and covered with crusty white stuff, the stars so bright they hurt the eyes. Everywhere, the whisper of demon minds.

I was afraid. I wished I am home.

"You never showed it. You were so brave."

I sit down then and dream of Mythrin. In my dream, I am not alone. I have a friend.

"That was me. I guess our minds got a little mixed together then, eh? You knew I had the ring."

I knew but I could not claim it. You would begin to guess about me, and then you would hate me. The way your ancestors hated my ancestors. I did not want you to hate me. And so I put on your people's shape. Like costume. And then I wake up, and you are there.

"But you forgot the clothes."

I did not understand clothes.

"Why didn't you just look around in my head until you knew what was what?"

I am no Assassin!

"And you didn't *make* me like you?"

Anger. Hurt.

"Okay! Okay! I believe you!"

Happy.

"Well, I'm confused. Are we still dreaming? Or are we remembering?"

Yes.

"Mara? Do you have to go home? Can't you stay here?"

I must go. Here is a sign that I am true. A sign for you to hold, and to give back. I go tomorrow at noon.

"What sign? What do you mean? Mara?"

§

"So then I woke up, and I was in my bed. And this was in my hand." Ammy unzipped a hip pocket in her jeans and pried out something that winked red in the morning sun. She held it out on her palm.

"The ring!"

"The ring of the Urdar chiefs. Probably the most important thing in her whole world. And she gave it to me to keep for her, till she leaves. To show she trusts me." She pushed it down deep in her pocket and zipped the zipper.

They had just climbed down out of Founders Tower. That had been the first thing Ammy wanted to do when she woke up, even before breakfast — go and check on Mara — but they couldn't have rushed off like that without a lot of hard questions from Celeste.

Mara wasn't in the tower.

Simon pulled his hat down over his ears and his mitts up over his wrists and started down the hill, picking his way between the crusted, icy ridges and the deep, snow-filled pits. "You still haven't told me what Mara *is*. Guess that means you don't trust me."

"I do trust you. She asked me not to tell anybody." Ammy crunched and slithered beside him. "She's sure people will hate her and try to kill her if they know what she is."

"Well, that sure makes me feel better! Why aren't you scared?"

"Because she's…" Ammy balanced on the edge of a long, icy patch and took a deep breath. "She's amazing. I wish I could be like her."

"Anyway, *I* wouldn't hate her."

"It's not up to me. Whoo!" She slid down the icy patch on her feet, spreading her arms for balance.

Simon detoured around. "So, it's all over today at noon. Things are already starting to feel normal again."

"For you, maybe."

"You know what I mean. And without Mara's book, there'll be no way to prove there's more than this." He waved at the snowy roofs ablaze with sunshine below them, the hard blue sky, the cold, real world. "Maybe one day I'll wake up and think all that stuff with Mara never really happened."

"I won't. I'll never forget Mara. Never!" She dug her chin into her scarf. "I wish I was going with her."

"What?" Simon grabbed her by the arm before

she could slide on down the hill. "You don't really mean that!"

"Why not? It wouldn't be forever. Just a visit." She yanked her arm away.

"But you can't!"

"What's the matter with you?" She shaded her eyes at him. "You should be begging to come with us! I mean, yesterday we missed the chance to see a new world. Didn't that just kill you?"

He couldn't believe what he was hearing. "Yesterday we almost got killed! By something that came out of Mara's world! That wanted us for dinner!"

"Stop yelling!"

"I'm not! Who knows what else we'd find there?"

"But that's the whole point!" She hacked at the air with her hands. "Nobody knows! *Think*, Simon!"

"No, *you* think."

"A whole new world, and we'd be the first human beings to set foot on it! How could you turn that down? Besides...." She lowered her voice to normal and smiled. "We'd be with Mara. We'd be safe with her."

He made a fist and thumped his forehead. "You are so... What do we know about Mara? What do we know about this world of hers — what did she call it, Merthin? Methrin?"

"Mythrin!"

"Okay. She was chased out of there, remember? She's in some kind of war with her brother. And after she looked in that book she said, 'My people are dying.' Ammy, use your head! If you think this would be like a trip to Peru with your parents, you're nuts!"

"Huh, some scientist you are," she sneered. "I bet your Carl Whatsisname would've jumped at the chance."

"He would not. That's not how scientists work. They don't jump. They *observe*."

"Yeah, well, observe this!" Ammy stuck out a boot and swiped his feet out from under him and down the hill he went. He grabbed her ankle as he fell and they both rolled over and over down the steep slope, flailing and kicking, spraying snow.

At the bottom Simon lay flat on his back a minute with all the breath squashed out of him. Then he sat up and scooped snow out of his collar. "What was that for?"

Ammy was laughing. "That was for going all stuffy on me." Her eyes shone and her cheeks were apple red. She looked wholesome and happy and even festive, with snow sparkling in her flame-coloured hair. He almost told her so, but knew she would have hated it.

He scrambled up. "Want to go over to Ike's place? We could play video games."

"Video games? Puh-leeze!"

"Shame to waste a nice morning like this doing nothing. Five more days till school starts."

Ammy shuddered. "You had to remind me!"

All the way home Simon tried to tell Ammy about Dunstone Public School. "You'll like it," he told her. She didn't look convinced.

"You, um, weren't serious back there, were you? When you said you'd like to go with Mara?"

"Darn right I was serious." She laughed. "Oh, don't look like that! She'd never say yes."

§

Back in the apartment, Amelia went to her room and opened her laptop. There was a new message from her parents. It sounded as if her mother had written it, and her father had gone over it afterwards and put in a few funny bits. Summed up, it said that Amelia was to act her age and not fly off the handle over every little upset, and she was to write out in careful detail exactly what was bothering her and then they would go over it with her and work out how to deal with it. *And don't forget your grandmother is there and she's a wonderful listener.*

Amelia read over the message she'd sent them last night, and her face reddened.

Dear Mom and Dad, she typed, *forget that last email. Things aren't so bad here. In fact, some things are pretty good. I have a new friend. Maybe I can tell you all about her soon.* She wondered if she would really be able to tell them all about Mara, ever. All the same... *I think I might be okay here*, she typed.

§

Simon went and threw himself down on his bed. There was too much to think about. Mara, and the Book of Lands, and the Assassin, and the blue door, and the library — or was it a museum? — and the smell of fresh air from another world, and the whatever-it-was that stole the book last night and then just flew off with it, apparently, and now Ammy...

He sat bolt upright. "Ammy!" That's right, that came first. He wouldn't put it past her to try to run away with Mara, just to get out of that first day of school. And he wouldn't put it past Mara to say yes. So the big thing was to figure out how to save Ammy from herself, *then* think about how the entire history of the human race had changed. He flopped back on the bed.

But save Ammy how? What could he say?

Celeste would know what to do. "If only I could tell her everything!" He'd promised not to. But that didn't count any more, did it? Mara was in no danger now, at least not in the kind of danger they'd thought at first. And they'd told Ike. Telling Celeste couldn't hurt Mara and it might help Ammy.

When the door opened and Celeste came in, he made up his mind. She sat on the edge of the bed and smoothed back his hair from his forehead, like she used to when he was small. He told her the whole story, starting from the minute the three of them started up Riverside Drive that first evening. His eyes were half closed and Celeste was a comforting shape against the light, a shape that made encouraging noises and didn't interrupt. She stroked his forehead. His thoughts whirled slower and slower and finally spun to a stop.

§

"Hey there, Rip Van Winkle! Planning to sleep all day?" Celeste grinned at him past the open door.

Simon sat up and rubbed his eyes. "What time is it?"

"It's half past eleven! How's your appetite? I bought roast beef sandwiches at the deli. I've been working like a fiend all morning and I'm starving!" She vanished from the doorway.

Simon shook his head. Something funny there. She was too ... well, too normal. Like he hadn't just told her all that amazing stuff. "Celeste!" He got up and lurched down the hall to the kitchen. "You were up here a while ago." She looked at him blankly. "Weren't you? We talked, right?"

"You must've been dreaming, my lad."

But he knew that hadn't been a dream. He went back to his room and looked at the dent in the quilt where somebody had sat beside him and smoothed his hair. Somebody. Not Celeste. Then who?

CHAPTER TWENTY-THREE
A CAP OF FEATHERS

Ammy was gone, too. A yellow sticky note stuck askew on her door. *Mara phoned,* said the note in a scrawly handwriting. *She wants the ring now. I'm taking it to her in the tower. Amelia.*

Simon ran back to the kitchen. "When did Ammy leave?"

"Haven't seen her. Why?"

He dashed to the front door and out, grabbing coat and boots in passing. Celeste called after him, but by then he was halfway down the stairs, hauling on his boots in mid-step, clutching the banister to keep from pitching down.

He ran straight into Ike, who was just stepping out of the *Independent* office. Simon grabbed his arm and urged him around the corner and northward. As they thudded along Wallace Street and up Hill Street, Simon gasped out the story. They turned right at the entrance to Founders Park and headed straight up the hill towards the tower. The slope and deep snow and breaking crust slowed them to a trudge.

"That had to be the Assassin, disguised as Celeste," Simon said between puffs. "He knows Ammy has the ring. He wants the ring. And he found out Mara's planning to leave at noon."

"So the phone call Ammy got was him?"

"Had to be. He's used the phone before. Mara never did."

Simon had no idea what he expected to see in the tower. There hadn't been time to think. He had a vague picture in his mind of Ammy backed against the parapet at the top of the tower, clutching the ring and daring the Assassin to try to take it off her. He looked up as they reached the crest of the hill, but nothing showed between the arches under the conical roof.

He was two strides away from the bottom of the tower when Ammy stepped out. He stopped short. Ike piled into him.

"Ammy! You okay?"

"'Course I'm okay. Why not?" She laughed at them over layers of red scarf. "You can have the book back, if that's what's got you worried. It's up there." She waved a hand upward.

"You found the book? But how?"

She didn't answer, just walked past them and started down the hill.

Ike dodged around Simon and charged into the doorway and up the stairs. Simon looked after Ammy. She seemed all right.

Somebody screamed at the top of the tower. Then, "Simon! Simon!" By then Simon was halfway up.

When he reached the top he had to push past Ike to find Ammy. She was lying on her back, hands crossed over her stomach, eyes closed. He fell to his knees and reached out a trembling hand to push the scarf back from her face. Her cheek was warm.

"Is … is she…" Ike stammered.

"She's alive. Ammy!" Simon shook her. Her head wobbled back and forth like a doll's.

"What's the matter with her?"

"I don't know! It's like she's asleep, but…"

"And," Ike squeaked, "and who was that down there that — that looked like her?"

"Who do you think?" *Wake up, Ammy!* "We already know he can change how he looks."

"Then that must have been him last night, up on the school roof. The one who took *this* off us." Ike pushed at something with his foot. It was the Book of Lands. It lay open against the base of the parapet, a foot or so from Ammy's head. A charred square hole ran all the way through the pages from front to back. All the coloured squares had been destroyed.

Simon remembered when Ammy read the book — how her mind had seemed lost in the squares. Suddenly, what was happening dawned on him, and his face paled.

"She's in there." Simon whispered. "Her mind. He took the ring, and then he put her in one of those squares, and then he fixed it so her mind can never get out."

"What are we going to do?"

"Call an ambulance. ... No, that won't help." Simon scrambled to his feet and looked out over the parapet. He had to search for a moment in the blaze of sunlit snow, but then he found it: a small figure marching briskly across the park. It stepped onto Hill Street and turned left.

Time? His watch said 11:48. At twelve, Mara would be gone. Or maybe dead, if the Assassin got to her first. "Mara. She might help. She has to help!" Simon tore off his parka and draped it over Ammy's body, with its jeans and useless little leather jacket.

Ike crouched beside her. Tears dripped off his chin.

"Try and keep her warm!" Simon said. "If I'm not back by..." Time. Time ran differently there. Time might save Ammy. "By half an hour, get her to a hospital."

He nearly fell on the stairs. At the top of the hill he flung himself down and rolled. It was the fastest way down. At the bottom he leaped up and ran. The wind whistled through his sweater, but soon he was warm enough not to feel it. His boots weighed like lead on his feet. At the bottom of Hill Street he kicked them off and raced on in his good, thick, water-repellant wool socks. Shouts followed him. He ran a red light where McNairn met Queen Street, dodged a turning tractor-trailer, raced on to a chorus of blaring horns.

On the Queen Street bridge he hung on the parapet, gasping. Eastward, a dark figure walked along the brink of the gorge. It started to pick its way downward.

Simon dared a glance at his watch: 11:56.

He sprinted. Slipped in the slush at the end of the bridge, went down flat on his back in the middle of the road. Staggered up, sprinted on along the cliffside trail. Reaching the path that angled down the side of the gorge, he went down it in leaps, grabbing at the elastic cedars and throwing himself from branch to branch. At the bottom he had to slow down and watch where he was going or risk breaking an ankle, and then where would Ammy be?

In sight of the cave mouth now. Somebody was climbing over the lip of the ledge.

11:59.

Later, he remembered almost nothing of the next minute.

The rocks in the cave mouth were blue with reflected light when he pulled himself onto the ledge. He flung himself down and wormed his way into the inner cave. No Mara. No Assassin. A tunnel of blue light bored into the solid rock. He jumped for it.

§

The tunnel emptied Simon out onto the triangle of bare red-brown floor in the library. He was alone, but footsteps sounded not far away. He got up and followed them, silent in his damp wool socks. His wet sweater and shirt clung coldly to his back.

"What's all this stuff doing here, anyway?" said Ammy's voice, suddenly so close that Simon jumped. "Like, what's that for?"

He pushed apart two tall steel-bound books and peered through the gap between them. Mara and Ammy — or somebody who looked exactly like Ammy — stood on the other side of the row of shelving, with their backs to him. They were looking at a cap made of feathers, blue and purple and gold.

"Two different questions," Mara said. "This place has many doors, to many places. These things are ... what is word? Starts with *S*."

"Souvenirs," said Ammy-the-fake. "Samples. Specimens." Her — no, his — hand rose behind Mara's neck. Simon took a breath to call out, but then Mara turned around, and the hand fell.

"Yes, specimens."

"So, what is that hat there for? What does it do?"

"I think just to wear. It does not look dangerous." Mara picked the feathered cap off the shelf.

"Put it on! Just for a sec, eh? It'll look so pretty on you." Ammy-the-fake took the hat and stepped behind Mara. He set it on her head and smoothed Mara's tangled hair over her shoulders.

Mara stood perfectly still. Her face wore a listening look. The Assassin waved a hand in front of her eyes. Mara didn't move. His right hand made a snicking sound and shaped itself into a set of gleaming knives.

Simon yelled and pushed hard at the steel-bound books. They shot forward. The Assassin elbowed one of them away. The other one hit Mara in the side of the head and knocked the cap off. She staggered. Blades clashed inches from her neck. She whirled and lunged.

Simon couldn't see what was happening. He ran along the row, looking for a gap. Couldn't find one, so he ran back, climbed up onto the shelf, and wormed his way between the books.

When his head came out on the other side, he looked down on a tangle of bodies. The one on top still had Ammy's shape, but its back shone iridescent purple-green. Both of Mara's hands were locked around its neck. The knife-blade fingers snapped at her face.

Simon pushed himself all the way through. He fell head-first, breaking his fall with his hands and arms. Landed right next to the struggling bodies. A blade nicked his ear. He yelped, rolled away, came up against a shelf with his nose in feathers. Birds sang sweetly, someplace very near and beautiful but also very far away. He grabbed the feathered cap, rolled over again, and stuck it on Ammy/Assassin's head.

The struggle collapsed. Mara pushed the Assassin aside, sat up, looked into his blank face — he still looked exactly like Ammy — and bared her teeth. "He brought me the ring. He had Amelia's shape. Did he kill her?"

"No. But he did something else." Simon wiped blood from his ear as he told her about the burned-out book.

"We go." Mara jumped to her feet.

"Where? How can we find her?"

"He will tell us."

But when they looked at the floor, the feathered cap lay empty. Something silvery flicked out of sight through a gap between the books.

"Let him go! I will know where Amelia is when we are out of this place. Come!" The red angora sweater was torn and darkly smeared, but Mara moved with ease. Simon had to trot to match her long stride.

"Isn't it dangerous to let the Assassin run around loose?"

"For him, yes." Mara shook back her hair and strode on. "If we meet in my own country, in my own shape, I will bite him in half."

Simon needed almost all his breath to keep up with her, but he couldn't resist spending some of it on questions. "So your people use this place to travel around?" he asked, between puffs. "Visit different worlds, collect things?"

"No! Only the young, foolish ones come here to try the gates, to prove their courage. Most of them never return."

"But didn't your people make this place?"

"It was old before we came, and the things in it." She tossed the words over her shoulder at him but didn't break stride.

"What, even the Book of Lands?"

"Even that. We only put our sign on it."

"Ah. Um ... and you know about the time difference?"

"What time difference?"

"The difference in time between the worlds. Something like ten to one. You've been in our world three days, right? In your world it'll be more like a month."

"Month?" She frowned back at him.

"Thirty days."

Mara stopped dead and grabbed his arm. "This is true?"

"Close as I can figure."

"They will think I am dead!" She dropped his arm and sprinted. He raced to catch up.

They ran, dodged through gaps, ran some more. When they came to the head of the stairs Simon started down at once. He had reached the landing before he realized Mara was not right behind him. Then came a sound he remembered, the crunch and click of heavy, clawed feet. Only now the sound came from above him, not from below.

That's got to be Mara. It's okay. But his stomach tied itself into a knot and his heart tried to hammer its way out of his rib cage.

He ran down the stairs. Yellow light painted the walls. At the bottom, an arched opening framed a peach-coloured sky. Simon shot out of the door and skidded to a halt.

A breeze blew his hair into his eyes. The air smelled of warm stone and green, growing things. In front of him the stony ground slanted down a couple of yards and then ended. A big boulder stood on the edge of the drop. Much farther away and lower down lay a plain covered with long silvery grass. In the distance, red peaks and pinnacles rose out of a pinkish haze.

So this was it. This was Mythrin. The world of the Urdar. He caught his breath. "It's beautiful!"

He walked forward. And stopped short again as the boulder unfolded itself and turned a questioning head over a scaly shoulder. The scales were dark green. The eyes sparkled yellow. The jaws widened in a smile.

"One of the little demons!" Its voice was a velvety rumble. "Come here, tidbit." It turned its body all the way around and reached for him with a long-taloned paw.

Something hit him hard between the shoulder blades, knocking him flat on his stomach. A red shadow floated over him. A tangle of screams and snarls broke out, and then suddenly cut off. Silence then, except for a thrumming sound. He raised his head cautiously.

"Gone," said Mara. She purred like a houseful of satisfied cats. She turned her head over her shoulder on the end of a long, shining neck. "You are not hurt?"

There was no doubt about it now. In one far back corner of his mind the hints had been piling up, getting harder to ignore. But still it was a shock to see the truth for himself.

Mara was a dragon, and this was a dragon world.

CHAPTER TWENTY-FOUR
INTO THE JAWS OF DEATH

Simon got his feet under him and stood up, brushing dust from his clothes. Mara crouched on the very edge of the drop and gazed straight out across the plain, towards the hazy horizon. Her whole huge body was quivering.

This close, Simon had a much better view than he really wanted. Her skin looked like a flexible coat of armour made of overlapping ruby scales.

Each rear foot had four clawed toes in front and a fifth claw in the back. The front legs — no, they were more like arms — ended in five-fingered paws, with the thumbs curving in the opposite direction from the other four, like a human hand. Each claw was an inch thick at the base and narrowed to a point invisibly fine. The ring of the Urdar chiefs fit snugly on the left thumb, just above the claw.

"Can you … um … feel Ammy out there?" he asked, although he really didn't want to draw her attention.

Mara didn't look at him. "They are coming," she said in a deep, vibrant voice, like a cello.

Simon looked, but the only new thing out there was a wide band of cloud. It had to be cloud: a dark bar that crossed the sky from side to side as far as he could see. But it was rising fast, faster than any cloud should be able to move.

"They are coming! My people!" Wings, each bigger than the side of a bus, quivered along Mara's body.

The cloud was getting wider as it soared nearer across the sky. Not a cloud, Simon realized. Dragons. There must be hundreds of them. Thousands. All coming here.

"Why … what do they…"

"They know I am here. They come to meet me." Her voice dropped to a hissing whisper. "Or to kill me? I have been away so long. Will they think I deserted them?"

Her wings unfolded with a sound like silk sliding on silk. They arched above Simon, a crimson tent. The air glowed red beneath them.

"Mara, we've got to find Ammy!"

She turned her head and pinned him with her emerald eyes. "*You* must find Amelia."

"Me? By myself?"

"She needs me, I want to find her, but" — she hissed in and out — "my people need me. And there is war."

"I can see you're in a fix, all right. But how am I going to find her?"

"Look for a dragon that looks like Amelia."

"A what?" Simon nearly fell over. "You don't mean —"

"She is in dragon form. How it happened — I think the Assassin. A joke, perhaps."

"Joke!"

"The blame is mine. He could not have done it but for me. She shared my dreams."

He puzzled over that for two seconds, then put it away for later. "Where?"

"That way." Her head snaked out. "I think she is in Sissarion. Not good, if my brother still holds the city."

"Let me get this straight." Simon's legs folded up and let him down hard on the rock. "I have to go and get Ammy — who is a dragon — out of a city of dragons. Enemy dragons. And I don't even know which one she'll be."

"Look at the eyes. The eyes are the last thing to change."

"That's a big help." He dropped his face into his hands.

"Are you afraid?" A growl rumbled up her throat. "Then go back now."

"Of course I'm afraid!" His head snapped up. "But I can't go back without Ammy!"

"Find her, then. You speak of fear, but I know you are brave." She turned again and crouched. Then paused and spoke over her shoulder. "And go quickly! If my people find you here, they will take you for a demon. They will eat you."

With a downbeat of wings that blew Simon's hair into his eyes and sent pebbles flying, Mara leaped into the sky. He watched her soar towards the distant cloud. It was so close now, he could make out thousands of beating wings in a dozen different colours.

"Find Ammy, she says." He looked out over the grassy plain. Those pinnacles poking out of the pinkish haze over there, that was Sissarion, city of the Urdar. A good two hours' walk, he estimated, just to be somebody's lunch.

"Find Ammy. Right. And come back alive?"

He climbed to his feet and turned around. There in the cliff was the arched gateway. The way back. For a moment he wavered. It would be so easy just to run up those stairs, back through the library, back home. Home.

Where Ammy's body lay. Alive, but empty.

"Okay." He turned and looked down over the edge. "Now, how do I get down from here?"

§

Amelia called Mara's name twice, and then no more. The lingering echoes were her only answer. They gave her the creeps.

Where am I? she thought. *Too dark to tell. How did I get here?* That, at least, she could guess.

It happened so fast. Mara had met her eagerly at the top of Founders Tower. "The book?" She'd snatched it, thumped it down on the stone floor, and knelt to turn the pages. Then stopped and said, in a businesslike tone, "There. That one."

"That one" was a black square faintly streaked with stony grey. She'd grabbed Amelia's hand and slapped it down on the square.

Next moment — darkness. A white square stood within a leap or two. Amelia yelled "Mara!" and took two steps, then flinched back, an arm over her eyes, as the white square filled with roaring fire. Then it vanished.

Leaving her sure of only one thing: That had not been Mara on the tower.

She was afraid to move. She couldn't see her hand in front of her face: she'd tried. The next step, or the next, might drop her into a pit full of sharp rocks, or icy water, or ... or centipedes.

I may die here!

For a time that could have been minutes or hours — she had no way of measuring — she stood rigid.

Rooted to the ground, like a stalagmite. When that thought crept through her brain she guessed it was a message from her senses. *I'm underground. I'm in a cave. That's why there's no light.*

Cool air stroked her face. Air, moving ... it must be moving from somewhere. *All right*, she thought. Take a chance. Move in the direction the air's coming from. Maybe that will lead to the way out.

Holding her hands out in front, she slid her feet across the rough ground. Something small ran across one foot. She jumped back, lost her balance, and sprawled. She picked herself up, rubbed her bruised elbows, and found the direction of the air again. After that she tried not to think of what might be running around down there.

At last her hands met a stone wall. Feeling to the left, she found a smooth opening in the stone. She traced its shape: a low, narrow archway, just big enough to squeeze through if she stooped. *Yes! Civilization!*

Sounds came from beyond. She ducked through the archway and found a long, dim tunnel with a rounded roof. It would have been pitch-black to anyone who hadn't spent an hour or so in real darkness. The far end curved into a suggestion of light. She tiptoed as far as the bend. The sounds grew louder.

A space opened before her, huge and softly lit and full of movement. It made her think of Pearson

Airport, where she'd got off the plane from Vancouver, but four Pearson Airports would have fit in the space under this roof.

The light shone from an enormous archway in the left-hand wall. It was bright enough to kick gold and silver gleams from the polished floor. And to show... Amelia shrank back into the archway. Those things out there, they looked a lot like the shape Mara had taken when she first came out into Dunstone Gorge and started all this.

No mistaking it now. Dragons! There had to be a dozen — no, twenty, thirty. More! Bronze, steel grey, sapphire, shimmering sea green, shining inky black. Only a few red ones.

At least I know where I am, now. I'm on Mythrin. Unless there are other dragon worlds.

None of them paid her any attention. They were all stalking towards the enormous archway, which would be about a block away if she were in Dunstone, and probably about as high as the town hall. There were no other doorways, as far as she could see, except for the one where she crouched like a snail peering out of its shell.

More dragons coasted down from above and settled to the floor with a rustle of wings. Up in the roof was a hole that looked like the bottom of a tube. She guessed it was about as wide across as the Hammer Block.

"That means no way out for me," she muttered. "I can't join that crowd, and I can't fly!"

She was thinking of the darkness in the cave behind her, wondering if she could stand going back there to try to find another door, when one of the dragons wrinkled its nose, turned its head, and saw her. Its eyes flared like green traffic lights and it let out a sharp hiss.

Before she could squeeze back into the tunnel, clawed fingers caught her by the arms, dragged her out, and dumped her on the ground. When she looked up she was surrounded.

CHAPTER TWENTY-FIVE
THE LAST THING TO CHANGE

Simon watched the battle from above. Thousands of dragons wove patterns in the air, black against the red light shining from below. Between drifts of smoke, you could see that the fires had spread.

It had been easier to get into the city than he'd expected. The battle had emptied the buildings. For as far as he could see the sky was full of fighting dragons, and none of them had any attention to spare for a small creature crawling on the ground.

But he couldn't get into any of the buildings. Dragons had no use for stairs. All the openings were at the top, or dozens of feet up the sides. And down in the narrow, twisting, stony lanes, he couldn't see anything. No way he'd spot Ammy from there.

Which was why he'd climbed this hill near the city. If there was any chance at all he would spot Ammy, it would be from here. Behind him, a tall boulder stood against a rocky bluff. He could get behind that for protection, if he had to.

All the same, he kept his head down. Mara had said something about him to her followers, he hoped. Maybe none of them would eat him. But there was no way to tell who was on what side out there. They didn't wear uniforms or markers of any kind. He wondered how they could tell. Were they all mind readers?

More important: he wondered who was winning.

A cluster of shapes swirled in his direction: one enormous green-black dragon with three smaller ones close behind, red and gold and black. He pressed flat to the rock. The four of them hurtled over his head with a sound like four trains bursting out of a tunnel at once.

Simon clapped his hands to his ears, but he kept his eyes open. The cluster veered up the slope of the hill behind him and around its shoulder, and the roaring faded. Then a spout of flame shot up the sky from behind the hill. Three dragons, red and gold and black, flapped lazily back. They coasted down to join the hundreds of black shapes that swirled above the fiery plain.

He wondered if Ammy liked being a dragon. He wondered if she was still alive.

§

Voices wheezed and rasped at her. They were inside her head and outside at the same time.

"What is it?"

"A monster. Look at its eyes."

"A changeling!"

"A demon. Show us your true shape, demon!"

Amelia tried to stand, but a clawed hand batted her back down. She sprawled on her back. The dragons whistled. She thought they might be laughing.

She struggled up again. This time they left her standing. But she wasn't sure how long her legs would hold her up. All she could see was their eyes and teeth.

"Show us your true shape!"

"This..." Amelia whispered. "This is my true shape." She held out her hands, and then she saw.

Her hands were crusted with scales, brown with a dark red sheen. And tipped with claws. Her feet.... She looked down at them. Scales, claws. She looked back over her shoulder and found she could easily gaze back along her own backbone, all the way to the long, curling, barbed tail.

She must have made a sound, because the dragons were whistling again. Their eyes shone like emeralds and topazes.

"Chase it back where it came from."

"Skin it!"

"Drop it in the sea."

"Can it fly?"

"Fly, demon!"

"Quick! Or we'll eat you!"

The dragons crowded nearer. Amelia reared up on her hind legs and flapped her arms desperately. The dragons screamed with laughter. *Wings! Wings, not arms!* She tried to make her wings work, but nothing happened. It was like trying to flap her ribs.

"Enough! We are called."

The circle broke up. The dragons loped towards the enormous archway. Amelia stared. Were they actually letting her go? She drew a deep breath for the first time since they'd dragged her from the tunnel.

But two dragons still stood watching her. She took a small step back towards her bolt hole. One long arm flicked out and pinned her neck to the floor.

"Ow! Let me go!"

Each dragon grabbed one of her arms and leaped into the air. A sharp wind battered her. The floor sank, the cavern swung around dizzily, the ceiling rushed down at her.

Suddenly the walls of the tube were streaming downward all around her. And then they were gone. The sky opened above her, dark blue on one side, orange on the other, with a crescent of red sun showing on the horizon.

Tower tops dropped away below, and kept dropping. The grassy plain beyond the city sank into a red haze. She smelled a reek of smoke. Not wood smoke, more like a barbecue gone horribly wrong. The wind blasting downward all around her grew icy. The horizon spread wide, wider, and the sun crept up again.

Amelia's brain raced to figure how high she was, how many thousand feet. *So what?* she thought desperately. *I saw something like this before, flying over Saskatchewan. I felt safe enough then.*

Yes, but then I was inside a plane.

Both the dragons spoke at once. "Can it fly? Let us see!"

Amelia was too numb with fear to understand what was happening, not until they let her go. Then she heard only the scream of wind in her ears. Spread out below, in detail that grew clearer every moment, was the plain, a giant flyswatter swinging up to crush her.

§

Simon had no warning at all. One moment he was lying on his stomach, studying the flight patterns of hundreds of fighting dragons and trying to decide if any of them looked like Ammy in any way whatsoever. The next moment a dragon was settling onto the ledge beside him. It was bronze or yellow — hard to tell in the red afterglow of sunset — and its eyes were amber. It opened its jaws in a wide grin. Hot air rolled over his face.

Half a second after that, Simon was backed up against the bluff. Space gaped behind him: the crevice between the boulder and the hill. He pushed back into it as far as he could. His sweater stretched and ripped on the rough stone. It was farther than the dragon could reach, at least. It peered in at him but didn't try to claw him out.

Safe! And now what? Stay here till I die of thirst? Or... He remembered that hot breath. *Will it burn me out?*

Something brushed across his mind, cobweb-soft. The dragon's eyes brightened. "Simon," it whispered.

"How ... who...?"

"Don't you know me? Look!"

The dragon's outline melted. Its legs and body shrank, its head grew round, scales vanished into skin. What stood before him now was ... Ammy? But she was thinner and paler than he recalled. In fact, everything about her was more *something* than he recalled. Her black leather jacket was tight as a skin and glistened like a beetle's back. Her boots were enormous. Her hair stood up in fluorescent red and yellow spikes. Yellow eyes stared like muddy pools from the white oval of her face.

"Ammy?" Simon inched forward, but not all the way.

"Of course it's me. I'm not a dragon. See?" She held out her hands. "I need you to help me get home."

"Ammy! But you look so weird!" He struggled to pry himself from the crack. "Can't ... seem ... to get my foot ... ugh!" He yanked, but only hurt his ankle.

"Let me." Ammy crouched, reached into the crevice, and pulled Simon's foot free. Then she took hold of him under the arms and pulled him out like a cork from a bottle. She turned, lifting him, put her back to the crevice, and set him down on his feet. *Being a dragon must have left her extra strong*, he thought. She couldn't ever have lifted him before.

It occurred to him, as distantly as if somebody was shouting at him across a football field, that he wasn't being very bright.

Sharp nails dug through the sweater and into his skin. He shrank away from the hands and turned around. "Your eyes are all wrong." He stared at them and felt dizzy. He wondered if he was being hypnotized. "Ammy has blue eyes. They should be blue."

The eyes are the last thing to change.

"Those..." He couldn't stop staring. "Those are your own eyes, aren't they?"

"Uh-huh." She/it grinned and changed back to a dragon. The change gave Simon a moment to blink away from the yellow stare.

But it did him no good, because now the dragon was between him and the crevice. He had nowhere to go but over the edge.

§

Later, Amelia thought it was simple instinct that saved her. She flung out her arms and legs, flung out her whole self against the fall. And her wings, forgotten until now, swept out and cupped the air.

It was too sudden. She flipped, spun head over tail, and plunged downward.

Then spread her wings again and slid sideways over air that seemed to have turned to clear jelly. Close beneath, pinnacles of rock swept past. Another couple of seconds and those teeth would have made a meal of her.

Amelia trembled. She held her wings rigid, planing the air, but the rocks thrust up at her. She was sinking. Desperately, she beat at the air the way a drowning swimmer beats at the water. Up she shot.

Then down she sank again, and again she struggled upward. Down and up, down and up. *How do they do it? How did I do it in the dreams?*

She was on a downward slide when she cut into a column of warm air and felt it pressing up under her wings. She veered to stay inside it, and rose, spiralling up and up with magical ease.

Thermals! Of course! Like a glider! Warm air rises and helps gliders — and dragons — to fly!

She had it now. She banked and soared and circled. She swooped down at the red-lit hillside, veering off at the last moment. It was like a sky-sized game of pinball, with herself as the player *and* the ball. She whooped and shrieked and buzzed the hillside again.

Then flipped over with shock and zoomed back. Even in this light her eyes easily picked out the two facing each other on the hillside. One of them was a dragon, and the other, the one teetering with his heels on the edge, was —

"Simon!"

Amelia folded her wings and dove.

CHAPTER TWENTY-SIX
CHOICES

Caught between the dragon and a sheer drop, Simon was ready to grab any way of escape. When the dragon suddenly leaped backward, he didn't stop to find out what had startled it. He darted past it to the right and clawed his way up the slope.

A hideous uproar broke out behind him as he climbed. Snarls, growls, shrieks. It sounded like the dragon had found an enemy more its own size.

Good. Hope they both keep busy till I can get away.

But it was over in moments. Simon poked his head out cautiously from his new hiding place, behind a fold in the cliffside where some small, scrubby trees had taken root. The bronze dragon was flapping off into the darkening sky.

The winner perched on the edge of the chasm and stretched out its long neck to look down. It was smaller than the first one, with a dark red sheen on its brown scales.

While it crouched there he didn't dare move.

"Simon."

It was croaking his name. He watched it without moving a hair. It was still straining to see into the darkness below the cliff. It seemed to think he'd fallen. Why should it care?

Maybe it knows I'm up here. Maybe it's trying to trick me into coming out. But fool me twice, shame on me, as Celeste says.

He could have kicked himself for being so stupid. *I should have remembered they can get into your mind!* The bronze dragon had skimmed that image of Ammy from his memories, of course, and fed it back to him. It did it so badly, though. *I should have guessed!*

"Simon! Where are you?"

Strange, how forlorn it sounded. How familiar. He raised his head.

Simon! The cry rang through his mind.

As it crouched and leaped into the air, so did Simon. He vaulted over the fold of rock and skidded down the other side. "Ammy! Wait!"

But Ammy was gone into the dark. *One second too late*, he thought. *Just one second!*

"Ammy!"

With a billow of wind and a scatter of pebbles,

she was back. She looked exactly like a dragon as she crouched over him, clumsily folding her wings against her body. Exactly, except for the round, blue, human eyes.

"Ammy! It is you, isn't it?"

"I thought you were dead!" A raspy, hissy voice, but somehow it still sounded like her.

Simon wanted to hug her, which horrified him. What part of a dragon could you hug? He stuffed his hands in his pockets. "I thought I'd never find you! Come on, we've got to get back to the gate."

"What, already? I'm just starting to get the hang of this! Simon, I can fly!" She spread her wings and wafted dust into his face.

"Your real body," he said distinctly, "is back home. In Founders Tower. Ike's watching it. After half an hour, he'll go get an ambulance."

"Half an hour. That's…"

"About five hours in this place. I figure we've been here four hours at least."

"There'll be a big fuss."

"At least. They'll want to find out what's wrong with you. They'll stick needles in you and take your blood."

She groaned. It sounded like a rusty gate creaking at the other end of a hollow tube. "But I'll never have this chance again! To really fly! Simon, you don't know how wonderful it is! Besides" — she held out her clawed front paws — "I can't go back like this!"

"Well… Hey!" He laughed. "You're a dragon, right? That means you can change your shape! Just change yourself back."

"Change myself?" Her eyes brightened. "Of course! Um…" She set her long teeth and scowled, and for a moment she looked just like her old self. Simon held his breath. She strained, and strained, and then slumped. "I can't do it."

"You could if you really wanted —"

"No! Don't you understand? I was like this when I came and I'm stuck this way! I can't go back!" She crouched with her clawed hands wrapped around her head.

"Okay, stay calm. When we go home, you'll go back into your real body."

"But suppose I *can't* get back in my body? There'll be two of me. One of me in a coma, and the other one — They'll shoot me or put me in a zoo!"

Her head went up. A shadow swept over them and they both cowered.

§

A bubble of laughter broke into Amelia's mind. And a voice: *Why all the noise? The sky has not fallen yet!* The shadow settled, folded its wings, and became an enormous crimson dragon. It shimmered in the sunset afterglow as if it was wearing a sequined coat.

Amelia's jaw dropped. It was her first really good sight of Mara. That glimpse back in Dunstone hardly counted. She'd forgotten, or never known, how big she was, how beautiful. "You're all right!"

"Are you winning?" Simon asked, from back against the cliff.

"At first the battle hung on a claw. But we are gaining. We will win."

Simon edged forward. He seemed to think Mara might gobble him up. "How did you know we were here?" he asked.

"Half of Sissarion knows you're here!" Mara laughed. "Amelia was thinking as loud as a hatchling clinging to its mother's back!"

Heat crept up under Amelia's skin. "I didn't know I was doing it. And I was scared. Okay, I *am* scared. Why can't I change back to my own body?"

"To choose and change your shape, that is a thing you learn. It takes time. I can teach you."

"She won't have time," Simon cut in. "We're going home now."

"Just a min—" Amelia began, but Simon spoke across her to Mara.

"What will happen to Ammy's body, at home, if she doesn't get back?"

"It will die."

Die? No! I can't die!

Of course you can. Everyone dies. But if you stay here, you stay as one of us.

Oh... Amelia gazed at Mara, then glanced at Simon.

"What's going on?" he demanded. "Why are you staring at each other?"

"Mind talk," Mara said aloud. "I will explain. Amelia has two choices. She can return to your demon world and put on her little, weak human body. Or she can stay here and share the life of the Urdar. As my more-than-sister, my friend, honoured by all."

"But she can't!" Simon sputtered. "Ammy, you're human! You can't just turn into a dragon!"

"Well, it looks like I just did, doesn't it?" She shrugged her wings, then grimaced. Her stomach felt hot inside. "Mara, can I breathe fire?" She took a deep breath.

"With teaching." Mara's long-taloned paw whipped out and clamped Amelia's jaws shut. "Without teaching, you will burn out your throat. Promise not to try it." She let go, but her paw hovered near.

"I promise!" Amelia grinned at Simon, who had backed away again. "But as a dragon, I should be able to —"

"Young dragons take years to grow into their powers. Flaming, dreaming, changing shape, and all the rest they learn as they grow. You have learned nothing. As you are now, you are dangerous to yourself."

"That's not the point." Simon was back again. "Ammy, you don't belong here!"

"That's for me to say, not you. And it's *Amelia*!"

"Amelia." He flapped that away. "You'll be dead. Your parents will have to bury you."

That hurt. She turned her head away.

"You haven't really thought about this at all, have you?" He waved his arms, taking in Mara, the dragons sweeping past, the fires spreading on the plain, the ruby pinnacles of Sissarion. "You really think this is all there is to being a dragon?"

"I've flown, you haven't." She folded her arms across her scaly chest.

"Well, it's not all flying around and breathing fire. You think you could kill somebody?"

"Of course she could," Mara said. "Amelia is strong. Stronger than she knows."

"What's strong for a dragon," Simon said, "is not strong for a human."

"I honour a fighter." Mara dipped her head at him. "Even if he is beaten."

I can't decide. Amelia looked from Mara, huge and glorious and shining, to Simon, small and ragged and dirty. "I can't make up my mind!"

"There is one other thing." Mara picked up a

stone the size of Simon's head and rolled it around in her paw, sharpening her claws on it. "The gate will soon be gone."

"What?" Simon's eyes opened wide. "How?"

"My people are destroying it. Not the gate itself, of course, that is beyond our reach. But we will ruin its housing and bury the passage between worlds. We want no more of us exiled ever again."

"But how will Simon get home?"

"There is still time, if he goes now." Mara smiled down at him. "I will take him there myself."

This time he didn't back off. "I told you before. I won't go without Ammy."

"Then stay here." Her smile sharpened. "But I cannot protect you, and who of the Urdar will believe you are not a demon?"

"That's not right!" Amelia flared up. "Of course he'll go home. *I'll* take him to the gate."

Mara looked at her. Her eyes shone in the semi-darkness like green lamps. "And then you will return?"

"I ... I don't know. I still can't decide."

Two dragons swooped overhead, shrieking. Mara's head went up. Amelia heard it too. "They've got him," she told Simon. "Her brother. They've captured him."

"Then the war is over?"

Mara unfolded her wings. "The war will be over when he is dead."

"Wait!" Amelia sat up on her hind legs. "You can't kill him!"

"It would be wise to kill him. I have learned that much."

"But you can't! Your own brother?"

"You have strange ideas, Amelia." Mara put her head on one side and narrowed her eyes. "Perhaps I will just bite his wings off and let him live on as a fearful example."

Amelia shuddered. "Is that a joke?"

"No. Now I must go."

"And I'll take Simon to the gate."

"Yes, go. Go and return." Mara spread her wings, leaped from the ledge, and was gone.

"Hurry!" Simon touched Amelia's forearm.

She had a horrible tight feeling in her chest. She stopped watching the sky where Mara had gone, crouched down, and stretched out her neck. "Climb on."

Chapter Twenty-Seven
The Burning Mountain

Gingerly, worried he would hurt her, Simon stepped onto Ammy's forearm and climbed astride the base of her neck, just above the spot where the wings joined the body.

"You sure you can carry me?"

"Just hold on!"

He wrapped his arms around her neck. The scaly skin was surprisingly warm. Muscles moved beneath it, wings swept out, and Ammy stepped off the ledge.

Simon's heart squeezed into his throat. They were falling, they were both going to be killed!

The next moment his hair flattened to his head as they bottomed out and veered upward. He gazed down at the distant plain, black with a red mottling of fire.

Higher and higher they rose, soaring in widening circles, and then Ammy broke from the spiral and flapped towards the mountains. Simon's whole body tingled, and he realized she was humming inside her dragon chest — a deep and wordless song of excitement and joy. And he was humming too.

We're both glad not to be dead, I guess. But no, it was more than that. *I understand, now. It would be awful hard to let this go.*

Awful hard, came her thought in his head. Then, *You think too loud.*

He pretended he hadn't heard. "How can we find the gate?" he yelled into the wind. "It's too dark! There's no moon!"

"... general direction ..." Her words came back in tatters. "... circle ..." Then she banked sharply to the right. Miles ahead, a plume of flame shot up from a fold in the mountains.

"Is that it?" Simon yelled.

She didn't answer, but her muscles strained. The wind of their speed tore Simon's ragged sweater half off his back. The closer they came, the higher the flames rose.

"There's the way in!" Ammy shrieked.

Simon could see it too, the rocks glowing red in the light of fires burning on the slope above the pillar-framed opening. All the side of the mountain was cracked, and flames shot up through the cracks, not just red and gold but green too, and blue, and a strange dusky purple.

As they watched from their circling height, the lines of fire ran together and the ridge above the gateway caved in. Fire exploded upward. The pillars cracked and fell. The whole mountain was burning.

That library, Simon thought, or was it Ammy's thought in his head? It must have been huge, it must have been the whole inside of the mountain. And now they're destroying it, all of it. Tons of books and weird specimens and strange machines, strange words and thoughts.

He thought of those mice from the silver box. He hoped they'd already got out.

And then he thought: *The gate! It's under all that. I'll never get home now.*

Wait. Ammy's thought. *Something's happening!*

Simon stared down at the mountainside. *What could be worse than this?*

Not there. There!

Then he saw it too. Shapes were forming in the black sky above the ruined mountain. Drifts and swaths of gauzy blue smoke. They rose, steadied, grew solid, took shape. Doors. Tall rectangles, each with an arched top.

Not just one door. Dozens.

Hundreds, came Ammy's thought. *Maybe thousands.*

The colour of the doors deepened to sapphire. Vines or root shapes twined across them. They hung there glowing, their bases just above the flames, their tops just below where Simon and Ammy veered in tight circles. A forest of blue glass slabs stretching as far as they could see.

"What the heck?" Ammy hissed.

"Ours wasn't the only one," Simon shouted against the wind and the roar of flames. "Mara said there were many doors, to many places. It was a kind of cosmic Union Station, I guess."

"So which one's ours?"

For one instant the doors hung there, solid as if they were truly glass, blazing like the sun was behind them. And then, instead of deepening into a thousand beckoning passages, they began to fade.

No! The thought came from them both.

"Which one?" Ammy screamed.

"Over there!" Simon pointed. One of the gates was different, because a large, silver-grey dragon was circling around it. "It's the Assassin! And he's got a grudge!"

§

The Assassin. Amelia was pretty sure he was the one who'd tricked her into the book. Maybe her being stuck in dragon form was his idea, too. And maybe he'd find out it wasn't such a smart idea, not for him.

"So that's what he really looks like. Well, he'd better sharpen his claws. Hold tight!"

"Ammy, no! You can't fight him!"

"The gate's fading. No time!" She rose, veered, folded her wings, and dove. The door swooped at them, larger and larger, the broken rocks showing blue behind it.

The Assassin reared up in front of the gate, huge wings outspread.

"Ammy, we'll never get past —"

She had a spectacular view of jagged jaws opening impossibly wide right in front of her.

Let go! A heave of her shoulder, and Simon went flying. Past the gaping jaws, straight through the blue door.

§

Red light, a roaring in his ears, heat on his back. All happening at once. A scream behind him, and a noise like shattering glass and a blinding burst of sapphire light.

He fell and fell down an endless, shining blue tunnel. The scream echoed and faded.

§

The heave of the shoulder that sent Simon crashing through the door also sent Amelia — not yet the most skilled flyer — twisting through the air. A blast of fire roared past her. She corkscrewed, all claws out, and clamped onto the first solid object she met. Something screamed with rage.

The Assassin. She was velcroed to the back of his neck. *The very last place I want to be!* He tossed his head back and forth to get rid of her. She slid and gripped again, and found herself hanging from his neck like a pendant on a chain, with her jaws up under his chin.

Now's your chance, called a distant voice. *Bite!*

The Assassin hurled himself through the air, looping and backflipping, trying to break her grip. She dug her claws in and held tight.

Now, Amelia, now! It was Mara's voice in her head, less faint, clearer. *Kill him!*

She could have done it. Something inside her, something that hadn't been there before, knew she could do it. Her jaws were easily strong enough to crush out his life through the soft spot under his chin, his one vulnerable spot. But...

I can't!

You must! Mara sounded closer.

But I —

That was when he pried her off and sent her spinning through the air, head over tail. With each spin she glimpsed his jaws opening wider, wider. Another two seconds and she would have got control of her flight path, but she didn't have two more seconds. Not even one.

Fire filled her world. After that, all she felt was colours. Burning red all through her body. Her mind awash with poison green: somebody's hatred.

Then the colours squeezed smaller, smaller, and then there was only a bright dot that winked out.

***

Simon sprawled with his cheek pressed on gritty ice. A shaft of light from above hit him in the eyes. He sat up, blinking.

"I'm home!"

He was lying on the floor of the cave in Dunstone Gorge. He was freezing. Something smelled like burned wool. "Ammy?"

He was alone.

Ammy didn't make it.

For long minutes he curled himself up around the memory of that scream. The dragon fire must have just missed him. It couldn't possibly have missed Ammy, the size she was.

It's so unfair! I mean, she wasn't even really there! How could she die there when her real body was here?

He sat up. "That's right, how could she?"

There's still a chance.

He staggered to his feet, cracked his head on the overhanging rock wall, fell down, and crawled out of the cave. On the ledge he squinted against the glare. A razor-edged wind sliced through what was left of his sweater. A big charred patch hung loose on one side.

By the time he was down from the ledge and halfway along the gorge to the path up to Deacon Street, his socks were crusted with snow again and his hands and ears were aching. He didn't care. *One chance*, he thought, over and over. *One chance*.

Chapter Twenty-Eight
Between

"What the heck? Where am I?" Amelia paused with her foot on the next step and her hand on the railing. She stood midway up a flight of stairs built of smooth white stone. The chrome railing was cold under her hand. "Mara? Mara! Where —"

"Well fought!" said a voice beside her.

"Mara?"

"Who else?" Mara took hold of Amelia's arm and urged her up the stairs.

"But you're not a dragon!"

It was Mara of the tangled dark red mane, Mara of the red angora sweater and long jean-clad legs. She was even wearing the sequined coat. Amelia looked down at herself. "And look at me. I'm human too. And ... oh, holy moly!" She stopped again and gazed around.

Stairs, stairs, stairs. All going in different directions, zigzagging across this gigantic stairwell that went down forever, or at least as far as she could see. It was dark down there.

And above her head, more stairs climbing to catwalks linked to corridors with open archways along them, which fed into closed corridors, which came out into catwalks and more stairs, stairs, stairs. All of it the same smooth white stone with flashes of chrome, all of it beautifully built. And most of it impossible.

Like that catwalk over there that started horizontal and suddenly went straight up.

And above her head, a flight of stairs came to a landing and headed off again in a different direction, upside down. Amelia pressed a hand to her stomach. "I feel sick."

"Don't look, then. Climb!" Mara pulled at her arm to get her going.

"What is this crazy place?"

"This is the dream between life and death. I *think*. It is the first time I am here."

"But what are we doing here?"

"I am here because you need me. You are here because you are dying."

"Dy— Wait a minute!" Amelia stopped again. "I thought I wasn't going to die in your world."

"That was before you chose to fight the Assassin. Your body lies broken and burned on the mountainside. I came too late. The Assassin, he lies there too," Mara added matter-of-factly. "We met and fought and he is dead."

"So I'm dead?" Funny, she didn't feel scared. Miffed, but not scared.

"No, not yet. If you come back with me there will be pain, but we can heal you. Come." She gave Amelia a push. "We must find the way back. And quickly!"

They reached the top of the stairs. A catwalk led off across empty space. Halfway along, it took two or three sharp angles and bent completely around itself, but that didn't seem to bother Mara. Amelia kept pace. The angles unfolded ahead of them. When they reached the other side, she didn't dare look back.

"So this is the dream between life and death. Why does it look like this?"

"Dreams are truth, especially this one. And it is your dream."

"I must be awfully confused."

Mara headed up another flight of stairs. Amelia trotted up after her. One good thing, you didn't get tired here. She must have climbed hundreds of stairs already and she wasn't puffing.

"So, you still want me?" They rounded the stair

head and turned into a corridor that corkscrewed into the distance.

"You are honoured with us. You are among the bravest of the brave."

"What — because I fought the Assassin?"

"Yes, and he with three times your size and ten times your skill."

"But that wasn't brave, that was … I dunno. Desperate. I just had to. Maybe if I'd had time to think about it first — but I didn't."

"Only one thing I do not understand. Why did you not kill him when you had the chance?"

"I … well … I couldn't."

"Why not?"

"Well, because … I guess I…" She slowed down and stared thoughtfully into the distance. That didn't help. She shut her eyes and hunted for the right words. When she opened them, Mara was tugging at her arm again. "I mean," Amelia said, as she started along the corridor, "I could've killed him but I couldn't have brought him back to life again, you know? I mean, it's forever."

"But he was trying to kill you."

"Right, but up to the last second I'd be looking for another way out. You see? So I wouldn't have to…"

Mara looked back at her, shaking her head. "This makes no sense to me."

They went on walking. Amelia's throat was too tight for words. After a few minutes she said in a blurry voice, "I wish I could make you understand."

"I too." Mara sounded sad.

No tears. Amelia tweaked her leather jacket. "Huh! If this is my dream, you'd think I'd dream myself a dragon, wouldn't you?"

"If you could, of course. Who would not?"

"But I didn't. So I suppose that means — that means — I'm not a dragon. Not really."

"No, you are not. If you had stayed with us, perhaps it would be different. But you must be true to your people, as I to mine." Mara took a look back over her shoulder and walked faster. She'd been doing that a lot.

"Why are we in such a big hurry?"

"Look back and you will see."

Amelia looked back. The end of the corridor was gone. A few yards behind them the stone walls and floor and ceiling were fraying, inch by inch, into blackness. The blackness crept nearer as she watched. "What is that?"

"The end of the dream."

This time Amelia didn't need to be pulled. They ran. There was something about the creeping darkness that made her go cold inside. "Why is this happening?"

"This is an in-between place. It cannot stay."

"What — what happens if the darkness catches us?"

Mara didn't answer, just ran faster. They ran and ran, and the darkness crawled behind them, slow, yet never far behind, swallowing up the corridors and catwalks and stairs.

At last they come to a wide hallway with two openings halfway along, one on the left, one on the right. Stairs led down from each doorway, came to a landing, and disappeared around the bend. Mara stopped between them. "This must be it. The place where you choose."

The two stairways looked exactly the same, except that a red light flickered deep down in the one on the right, and Amelia smelled smoke. The stairway on the left led down into a cool grey light, and the breeze that blew from it smelled like snow.

"One way leads back to your world, and one way leads back to mine." Mara stood at the head of the red-tinted stairs. "You know where I must go."

"And I..." Amelia looked from left to right and back again. Then back at the oncoming shadow.

"Hurry! If you wait too long, these will be gone. Only the third way will be open."

"What third way?"

Mara nodded with her chin along the corridor. It ran straight, with no more crazy bits. A few yards further on, it ended in a staircase that led up to a brilliant white haze. Amelia sniffed. Funny...

Mara's hand was on her arm. "No! That way is not for you, not yet."

Amelia had walked past the two stair heads and was gazing up into the shining haze. It wasn't really white, there were colours in it. And that smell... "Is that lilacs?"

"Amelia! That way leads to death."

She retreated to the space between the two stair heads. Three yards back in the direction they'd come from, the corridor was vanishing inch by inch. The darkness was so close now, she could hear a faint crinkling noise as the edges of the stone unravelled.

"How can I choose?"

"You have chosen. You know it."

"Yes, I know." Amelia threw herself at Mara and hugged her.

Mara hugged back so hard it hurt. "I knew you were my friend from the first moment, you with your head of fire. My first and only friend in a world of demons."

"Me too." Amelia held her off to look up at her. "Only, you do know my hair isn't really like this, right? It's just gel."

"Disguise. Costume. I know."

Amelia laughed. She scrubbed at her eyes with the back of a hand.

"No sadness," Mara said. "There are other doors, and maybe you will find them. You and —"

The crinkling noise was suddenly loud. She looked over Amelia's shoulder. The green shine in her eyes went dark. "Now, Amelia! Now!"

§

"Ike!" Simon yelled, halfway up the tower. "I'm back!"

No answer. He felt sick. When he flung himself up the last step and stumbled onto the platform, Ike was sitting beside Ammy as if he'd never moved. He looked up and shook his head.

"Is she… Has she…" Simon collapsed to the floor, panting, and crawled over to her.

"She's just the same. I'm scared she's…"

Simon knelt beside her, across from Ike. He held a hand close to her mouth. "She's still breathing." He touched her cheek. But so cold! "We'd better get her to a hospital. Call an ambulance. I'll stay, you go. Hurry!"

Ike sprang to his feet. He took one step towards the stairs, stopped at the sound Simon made, and turned back.

Ammy's eyelids flickered. Her eyebrows drew together. Her eyes opened. Simon let out a whoop. "You're back!"

"Yeah." She sat up stiffly. Simon's parka slid off her. "What's this for?"

"We had to keep you warm."

"Hypothermia," Ike began.

But Ammy wasn't listening. She put her hands to her face and burst into tears. Ike stood back, appalled. Simon, kneeling beside her, had no idea what to do, so he put his arms around her and squeezed as hard as he could. It didn't seem to help. She cried until she had nothing left but hiccupping sobs.

CHAPTER TWENTY-NINE
AMMY/AMELIA

"Hey! Ammy, can you do this?" Ike skated backwards in front of her.

"Go away, you're showing off." Amelia wobbled, flung out her arms, and just managed not to fall down, this time. Even Simon skated better than she did.

Roasted chestnut and french fry carts stood around the edge of the town hall square. Smells of coffee and fresh baking drifted from the doughnut shop. The sound system was playing the Blue Danube. The fresh snow sparkled like diamonds in the sunshine and everybody had rosy cheeks, not that Amelia was a big fan of the healthy outdoorsy look.

The rink was crowded, so there were plenty of people around to see what a dork she looked. If it weren't for that, she might've had to admit she was having fun.

Ike poked her in the arm. "I like the hair. It's cool. Well, cool-ish."

"Yeah, thanks." Yesterday evening, after taking a three-hour nap, she had washed the coloured gel out of her hair. It was back to its plain old brown, mostly straight but curling a little around her ears and on her neck.

"I like it," Simon said.

"The red and yellow wasn't me." She shrugged and nearly fell down again. Catching her balance she added, "It was what Mara said. A costume. A disguise."

Ike zoomed off again. Simon, wobbling along at her side, said, without looking at her, "So, do you really hate it here?"

"Oh, I don't know. I could get used to this town."

"I don't mean Dunstone. I mean Earth. You wanted to stay in Mara's world and be a dragon. You only came back by accident, when the Assassin got you."

"How do you work that out?"

"When you woke up, remember? I never saw anybody cry like that." He kept his eyes carefully on the ice ahead. "I won't forget how you made sure I'd get through. Even when it meant you ... you know."

"You mean, what I had to give up." *I spoke with dragons. I fought a dragon. I flew like a dragon. For just a little while, I was a dragon. Free, strong, magical.*

And it was all gone. Last night she hadn't even dreamed.

Amelia was tempted. She could let him go on believing it. He would owe her hugely for … well, maybe the rest of their lives.

She sighed. *Not dragon material, me.* "When I cried, that was for Mara. I missed her. I miss being a dragon too. But I'm back here because I chose."

"What, really?" He wheeled around, flailing his arms. His face lit up.

"Believe me. If I'd stayed on Mythrin it would've been a disaster. I didn't belong. Mara even said so."

"*Mara* said so? But I thought —"

"She said I have to be true to my people. That means my parents, and Grandmother, and you, and even" — she tipped her head towards the skaters — "them too, I guess, people I don't even know."

She waited for the big *Aha, told you so.* But it never came. Simon didn't even crack a smile. He just nodded solemnly and wobbled onward.

Go on, say it. You owe it to him.

"And you know what? I'd still be there, if you hadn't come in after me and tried to get me out. Sure, I would have figured the truth out after a while, by myself. But not till it was way too late."

"Oh. Good." Simon allowed himself a small, pleased grin.

"So, uh, I mean … thanks."

There was something else she had to tell him, but

before she could think how to say it, Ike came swooping in. He braked sharply in front of them, spraying ice. "Look, there's a bunch of kids over there who'll be at school with us on Monday. Let's go over."

Amelia looked between the whizzing skaters to a cluster of kids at the other end of the rink. Two or three of them waved. She waved back. "Who's the girl with the long black hair?"

"That's Dinisha." Ike elbowed Simon in the ribs. Simon's face went blank.

"Friend of yours?"

"Friend of Simon's. She's so smart she's scary. I mean, her project on genetically modified food took first prize at the Science Fair last year, *and* she's the captain of the girls' track team."

Simon cleared his throat. "She's nice, actually."

"Let's go over. C'mon!" Ike zipped away.

"You go too." Amelia wobbled to the bench at the side of the ice and started unlacing her skates. "My fingers feel like icicles. My ankles hurt. I hate skating."

Simon dropped onto the bench beside her. "Scared?"

She bent her head over the laces. Weird how they knotted just at the worst time.

"Um, I bet Mara wouldn't be scared." He was unlacing his own skates as he spoke.

She laughed shortly. "If Mara were ever afraid of anything, it would be this. Alone with strange kids at a new school."

"You won't be alone, Amelia. You've got me."

She looked up from the knot. He gazed down at her, skate in hand, solid as a truckful of rocks. "I do, don't I?" Then it hit her. "You called me Amelia!"

"It's what you want, isn't it?"

"Yes!" She worked off one skate, then the other, hauled her boots on, and laced them up with hard, determined jerks. "Okay, let's do this!"

She stood up, slung her tied-together skates over one shoulder, and settled her Peruvian hat on her head. As they started along the side of the rink together, she thought: *I'll tell him. Soon. But now's not the time.*

Mara's words hung glowing in Amelia's mind. *There are other doors, and maybe you will find them. You and...* That was for the future.

School, and Dinisha, and the rest of those watching, measuring eyes, they were enough to face for now. More than enough.

ACKNOWLEDGEMENTS

This book's gestation and birth were eased by the generosity of Marsha Forchuk Skrypuch (best of fairy godmothers) and the critical but kind attention of Erin Noteboom, as well as the Kidcritters of the CompuServe Literary Forum: especially Lynne Supeene, Amy Jones, Loraine Kemp, Rose Holck, and James Bow.